Praise for Surfing Detective Series

"Chip Hughes has captured the semi-hardboiled vernacular of the classic gumshoe novel, and given us an authentic Hawai'i, believable surfing scenes, good pidgin, and realistic local characters. Like a session in smooth blue water." *Ka Palapala Po'okela Excellence in Literature Award*

Murder on Moloka'i

"Hughes's pastiche of hard-boiled noir and the zen goofiness of surfing bliss is effortless and entertaining." *Honolulu Star-Bulletin*

Wipeout!

"Just right for the flight to the islands. Hughes's prose flows easily, slipping into Hawaiian pidgin when needed. His series remind[s] readers of a charming new *Magnum, PI.*" *Library Journal*

Kula

"Zips right along . . . pacing is first-rate . . . dialogue is snappy . . . strikes a nice balance between the Hawaii of today and the film noir memes of yesterday." *Honolulu Star-Advertiser*

Murder at Volcano House

"Glides along at a satisfying clip. The landscape and characters are consistently colorful. Hughes effectively uses the native Hawaiian language throughout and provides vivid descriptions of the legendary island scenery. Entertaining Hawaiian whodunit." *Kirkus Review*

Hanging Ten in Paris Trilogy

"What can be better than Paris and Hawaii? Three novellas working off of one another [in] a nuanced tapestry of layers [keep us guessing] right to the end. The whole trilogy [is] a page turner. Impossible not to enjoy!" *amazon.com*

BARKING SANDS

A Surfing Detective Mystery

Other Surfing Detective novels
by Chip Hughes

MURDER ON MOLOKA'I

WIPEOUT!

KULA

MURDER AT VOLCANO HOUSE

HANGING TEN IN PARIS TRILOGY

SURFING DETECTIVE
CONFIDENTIAL INVESTIGATIONS : ALL ISLANDS

BARKING SANDS
A Surfing Detective Mystery

CHIP HUGHES

SLATE RIDGE PRESS

Slate Ridge Press

P.O Box 1886
Kailua, HI 96734
slateridgepress@gmail.com

ISBN: 978-0-9992538-4-7 (print)
       978-0-9992538-5-4 (epub)
       978-0-9992538-6-1 (Kindle ebook)

First Edition 2021
© 2021 Chip Hughes.

Cover photo: Alvis Upitits

For Les Peetz

1949–2018

Jazz pianist, attorney, jokester, friend.

Acknowledgements

Many thanks once again to my wife, collaborator, and inspiration, Charlene Avallone; and to veteran Honolulu PI Stu Hilt; and also to Jana Argersinger, Lorna Hershinow and Laurie Tomchak, Miriam Fuchs Holzman, Glenn Stahl, Tim Hudak, a Kekaha, Kaua'i resident who wishes to remain anonymous, Cindy Inman, Michael Ives, Nathan Avallone, and Dr. Jill Portnoy, School of Criminology and Justice Studies, University of Massachusetts, Lowell.

We shall claim our lands from the Barking Sands
to the valleys of Hanalei . . .

—Dennis Pavao, *"All Hawai'i Stand Together"*

one

"It's about my daughter . . . Jennifer." She glances at coconut palms whispering in balmy trade winds outside my Maunakea Street office. "I'm Marian Reece, from Colorado Springs."

"Aloha, Mrs. Reece." I note her tarnished wedding rings. "I'm Kai Cooke."

She's a handsome woman—in her early sixties I'd guess from her silvering hair. Most of my potential clients remark on the sweet scent of plumeria wafting up from the *lei* shop below. She doesn't seem to notice.

"Why don't you tell me about your daughter?" I pull a yellow legal pad from the disarray on my desk and find a pen.

"Jennifer was one of three young women," Mrs. Reece continues as if on autopilot, "sexually assaulted and brutally murdered twenty years ago on Kaua'i by the Barking Sands Strangler." Her mechanical tempo suggests she's uttered these words a thousand times before.

"I'm so sorry." I take a closer look at her delicate features and see creases around her mouth and eyes that tell a story of pain, a story repeated in the somber eyes themselves. She clutches a tissue in one hand but doesn't seem to need it yet.

I glance down at the dusty linoleum in my Chinatown office above Fujiyama's Flower Leis. It's Halloween morning, I'm wrapping up an insurance fraud case involving a kite surfer, and I wasn't expecting visitors. Maybe an early trick-or-treater. But not a grief-stricken mother twenty years after her daughter's murder.

"Jennifer was a beautiful girl." Her cadence is more natural now. "Sweet and generous. Full of promise and ambition. She went to Kaua'i for an internship, caring for autistic children. She could have brightened many young lives."

"Her death must have been horrible for you." I lift my gaze from the floor and see again in her moistening eyes that story of pain.

"Not just for me." She raises the tissue and wipes away an expected tear. "It killed my husband. Four years after Jenny was murdered he died. He was only forty-three. He never stopped searching for her murderer. And he never moved beyond his grief. Grief caused his heart to stop."

I'm deeply moved by what Mrs. Reece is telling me. And, of course, I've heard about those unsolved murders on Kaua'i. But why is she here in my office?

Before she explains, she reaches into her purse and pulls out two photos of Jennifer: one in a bikini smiling on a sunny beach and the other a gauzy, airbrushed graduation portrait. Jennifer has chestnut hair that falls almost to her waist and eyes a delicate shade of green. Mrs. Reece's stunning daughter needs no airbrush. In both photos she wears a heart-shaped silver locket that her mother tells me was inscribed with the letter J.

"She's lovely," I say.

"So were the two other girls." Mrs. Reece reaches again into her purse and hands me photos of the other victims. "Tara Marie Havens and Elise Morneau."

I glance at the photos and slowly shake my head. Tara is a raven-haired, dark-eyed beauty barely more than a teenager and Elise is a bobbed blonde in her early twenties with a quirky smile. All three victims exhibit that proverbial flower of youth the Strangler no doubt craved.

Mrs. Reece explains that Jennifer was found above Waimea Canyon near Koke'e with the telltale signature of the Strangler. Then she produces another photo, a closeup of one of the victims, showing a crude line drawing of a breaking wave—a small squiggle consisting of thirteen cigarette burns.

"All three victims bore the exact same wave burned into their breasts," she says. "Until the brute is caught," her voice deepens, "I have made it my life's purpose to bring him to account. I can't say to justice because there could be no justice to answer for his crimes. Then I can die at peace and spend eternity with my Jennifer. My only child. Who will never be again."

Why's she telling me this? Again, I wonder but ask a less direct question: "What brings you to Hawai'i after so many years?"

"This is the twentieth anniversary of the Barking Sands killings. The anniversary has been widely publicized by Janson Newfield, an attorney running for the office of Kaua'i County Prosecutor. The election is only a few days away."

"I've heard of Newfield," I say. "He's proposing to crack down on that island's sex trade, saving Kaua'i from the massage parlors, sex clubs and street prostitution we have here on Oʻahu. Some people I know on the Garden Isle think Newfield's claims are overblown, even offensive."

"What I care about," says Mrs. Reece, "is Newfield's promise to solve several cold cases, including the Barking Sands murders."

"If he's elected, I hope he can bring you peace."

"His calling attention to Jenny's case may turn up new information." Her voice brightens. "When her remains were found in Waimea Canyon weeks after her disappearance police had little to go on. By then the Strangler had already killed the other two girls. He's never been heard from since."

"That was the strange thing. The killing simply stopped."

"Yes, unless we count the murder of a woman twice Jennifer's age ten years later."

"You mean Amity Johnson?"

Mrs. Reece nods.

"I remember hearing about her. When Amity Johnson was finally found her remains were too far gone to determine if she bore the Strangler's signature."

"Do you have children, Kai?" Mrs. Reece asks out of the blue.

I shake my head. "Afraid I'm too busy working and surfing to—"

"Let me tell you," she interrupts, "there's no love like the love for your own child. Having Jennifer was the best thing that ever happened to me. Losing her was the worst." Mrs. Reece pauses. "The thing that keeps me going is hunting him. Twenty years have come and gone, but I keep searching. Otherwise, I would wander through life aimlessly in my emptiness and grief."

"You're on a mission. And I can see why." But I'm still wondering where I come in. I don't have to wait long.

"I would like you to help me on my mission, Kai." She slows down and emphasizes each word. "I would like you to investigate my daughter's murder."

I'm speechless. Where to begin?

"What do you say?" The hopeful look in her eyes makes me wince.

"I appreciate, uh, your confidence in me, Mrs. Reece. But I doubt I could find much that Kaua'i police haven't after all these years. And I doubt they would cooperate with a PI, especially from another island. I don't want to waste your money on a false hope."

She's undeterred. "The odds may be long, but I don't care."

"Another thing, Mrs. Reece. I couldn't even start until I'm done with a big pending case."

"I've waited twenty years," she says. "I know how to wait."

Since trying to find a nice way to say no isn't working, I switch gears. "There are a half dozen private detectives on Kaua'i. I'd be happy to refer you."

"You come highly recommended. And you're a surfer. My daughter was a surfer."

"I'd like to help you, Mrs. Reece. I really would."

Her eyes are glistening again.

"I'm sorry." I rise from my chair, walk to the door, and open it slowly. I feel terrible. But what can I do?

She rises too, her lips pursed. She looks more determined than disappointed. Mrs. Reece steps through the threshold into the hallway, wipes another tear, then turns back and asks, "May I have your card?"

"Sure." I pull one from my wallet and hand it to her.

She glances at the full-color wave rider above the words—SURFING DETECTIVE: CONFIDENTIAL INVESTIGATIONS—ALL ISLANDS—and then into my eyes. "Thank you, Kai. I'll check back with you in a few days."

I nod. "I wish I could help."

She turns and marches resolutely down the hall.

two

Later that day I drive through Waikīkī. The surf is running about waist high. Conditions look clean and the little curls are foaming up to the oceanfront hotels. I pull into in the Honolulu Zoo lot, hike my board to the beach, say my surfing mantra, and paddle out to my favorite spot.

A couple hundred yards offshore of the Sheraton Waikīkī, far from more accessible breaks, Populars or Pops is a long paddle. Out here the water is a deeper blue and the swells come steaming in. Pops distance from shore keeps crowds small and mellow, except during a big summer swell. But now in late October—Halloween no less—the big waves have gone and so have most of the surfers. Good news. I don't like crowds. I think of myself as a soul surfer—a guy who surfs not for competition or glory or to be cool but for the love of riding waves.

When Hawaiians once lived on the oceanfront land where the Sheraton sits today, they called this spot Populars because it was their favorite place to surf. The reason they liked Pops back then, beyond its closeness to their homes, is the same reason surfers like it today: Pops serves up right-breaking curls that on a good day seem to sweep from here to eternity. As the waves peel and swing toward shore, they often bowl in sections. You can tuck into one of these turquoise dreams and ride all your cares away.

I could use a few rides like that today. The image of Mrs. Reece marching from my office still hangs in my mind.

Before long I'm in the lineup—all alone—and stroking for my first wave. I rise, tuck in, and ride nearly to the Pink Palace—the Royal Hawaiian Hotel. As I paddle back into the lineup, Mrs. Reece still occupies my thoughts. I feel bad about not taking her case. But how could I come up with anything new on the Barking Sands murders after two decades of police investigation?

Why she chose me I don't exactly know, other than I'm both detective and surfer. Oh, and highly recommended, in her own words. She may have found me on social media or my website, where I display the same gazelle-like hanging ten surfer as on my business cards and office door: back gracefully arched, knees bent slightly, arms cantilevered for balance, gauzy ocean spray enveloping board and surfer alike. *A thing of beauty.* An artist friend modeled the image after an unknown wave rider at Banzai Pipeline. I'd never claim to be as good as that guy. I'm a soul surfer, like I said. Well, I did compete once at Mākaha and brought home the third-place trophy that still sits in my Chinatown office.

My name—Kai Cooke—is inscribed on that trophy. Kai means sea in Hawaiian and Cooke comes from an old New England family. Though I can't claim native blood, I was *hānaied,* or adopted, by Hawaiian in-laws on my mother's side after she and my father were killed in a small plane crash when I was eight. Now I'm the proverbial age of thirty-nine, stand six feet even, and have sun-bleached hair from surfing. At work I wear an aloha shirt, khakis, and sandals. At play I wear board shorts. I try to keep a balance between the two. Work and play, that is.

Waiting for the next set to roll in, I consider what Mrs. Reece hopes to accomplish. Being in the water helps me think. Sherlock Holmes had his pipe—I have my surfboard. Floating on the glassy sea, scanning the blue horizon for the perfect wave, sometimes I drift into a kind of trance. From there I can disentangle the most intricate web. But it doesn't take a trance for me realize that what Mrs. Reece really wants is more than just to find the man who murdered her daughter. She wants to face him in court. She wants to tell him how he deprived her of her only child and of watching her grow into maturity and have children of her own—grandchildren for Mrs. Reece. Her daughter has been gone two decades while he has walked free. She wants him to pay. And even if the killer himself is dead, she wants to know he will never hurt another young woman.

I can understand her wanting these things. I can understand why she asked me to help. But she doesn't understand just how difficult it would be after all these years to turn up anything new. Especially without the assistance of law enforcement. The case has been cold so long and the evidence so carefully combed that nothing, or next to nothing, could be left.

Several more rides at Pops put me in a better mood. But when I finally paddle back to shore a little before sunset the smiling image of Jennifer Reece in her sun-soaked bikini follows me all the way in.

I haul my board out of the water, shower at Kūhiō Beach Park, and walk up Kalakaua Avenue in the glowing amber light past Waikīkī's oceanfront hotels. I'm dripping and shirtless. Some passersby give me a look. *The little pink welts on my chest.* I'm not showboating that halfmoon crescent of sixteen teeth marks. I'm not hiding it, either. Years ago a tiger shark attacked me on the North Shore at Laniākea. Fortunately, the shark didn't like the taste of me. He took one bite and swam off. Scarlet billows in the water scared the freaking daylights out of me, but nothing was broken except my skin. I paddled in under my own power, with an escort of surfers who couldn't believe their eyes. EMS gave me a ride to Kahuku Hospital. I got lucky. I didn't even stay overnight. But ever since that fateful day at Laniākea whenever I paddle out I pause, put my hands together on the deck of my surfboard, and say my mantra—*No Fear! No Fear!* Then I try to forget that shark. Otherwise, how could I ever surf again?

The sunset turns blushing peach, illuminating swarms of costumed characters on Waikīkī's sidewalks: Dracula, Madonna, Jack the Ripper, Father Time, Elvis, Little Red Riding-hood. *Halloween.*

A teenaged girl wrapped in a bedsheet dripping what looks like blood walks up to me and asks, "Guess who I am?"

She's wielding a plastic toy axe. And what's really weird about the red-stained sheet is the little boxes of individual-serving-size breakfast cereal attached to it.

"I give up," I say.

"A serial killer." She points to the boxes of toasted O's and frosted flakes and says, "Good thing you don't follow clues for a living. You'd go hungry."

Whatevahs. I start walking again. Serial killers aren't my *kuleana*—my thing. This teenager has reinforced my resolve not to take on such a case—especially one twenty years cold.

I proceed to the zoo lot, towel off by my car, pull on my khakis and aloha shirt, and head to Ah Fook Chop Suey House.

The Honolulu skyline is fading to pearly grey as I park in Chinatown and trek down River Street, curving along the shower-tree lined confluence of the Nuʻuanu and Waolani streams. Ah Fook is packed, as usual, a few diners and waiters in costume. I whiff the piquant aromas of steamed clams and Peking duck, then put my name in for a party of two. Despite run-ins with the health department and liquor commission, this little chop suey house can always be counted on for a good, cheap meal. If there's one thing my attorney friend Tommy Woo and I have in common, it's being cheap.

I step back out onto River Street where there is more elbow room. A century ago gamblers, smugglers, pimps, murderers, and thieves plied their trades on this notorious street along the riverbank, and legendary detective Chang Apana—model for the fictional Charlie Chan—hauled them in with his whip. He may have been stereotyped in the Earl Derr Biggers stories, but Chan's cleverness nonetheless earns him at least a few points with this PI. On River Street these days more homeless than criminals hang out—as elsewhere in Chinatown.

I check my watch. Seven, the appointed hour. No Tommy Woo. Tommy has his own version of Hawaiian time. Attorney by day, jazz pianist by night. How he manages to wrap up a late-night session in the wee hours, then cruise into his legal offices the next morning—eyes wide open—is a mystery to me. But if he can make it to his gigs and his office on time, why not to dinner with me? *Whatevahs.* I take my friend as he comes.

Just then the familiar lanky figure pops around the corner puffing cherry blend in his Meerschaum pipe. He joins me near the front of the lengthening line of waiting diners.

"Hey, Kai, it's Halloween." Tommy deadpans. "Did you hear the one about the two strippers who went trick-or-treating dressed as mermaid twins?"

"Haven't heard that one, Tommy." Over my shoulder I scan the waiting customers for ears too tender for one of his doozies. He's about to rattle off the punch line when we're thankfully called to our table. Tommy puts out his pipe.

As we step into the chop suey house Tommy brushes back the silver lock that perpetually droops to his tortoiseshell glasses, the kind Ivy League intellectuals wear. Tommy's father was Chinese, his mother Jewish, and he attended Jesuit schools. He cut his musical teeth on the jazz and blues of Duke Ellington, Charlie Parker, and B.B. King. A mutual friend once quipped that Tommy has the wisdom of Confucius, the funny bone of a rabbi, the pomp and circumstance of the Pope, and the musical soul of an African.

I don't know about that. But at the moment this unconventional genius is looking pale.

"You okay, Tommy?" I ask as we're seated at the table for two.

"Me?" Tommy sounds surprised. "Sure. Well, I've got a few complaints. Nothing serious."

"Like what?"

"A little short of breath and short on appetite. Sometimes a sore neck. Low fever. I'm just tired. That's all. My lawyer and musician gigs don't leave me much time for sleep."

"Don't know how you do it, Tommy," I say, smelling cherry tobacco wafting from his black shirt. "How about getting yourself checked out by a doc?"

"Don't trust 'em—any of 'em," Tommy replies. "Besides, once I catch up on my sleep I'll be shipshape."

A waitress steps up with two teacups and a steaming teapot. I pour and we both order the $10.95 dinner special.

When she departs Tommy, uncomfortable talking about his health, asks, "So what's new with you?"

I tell him about the insurance fraud case I'm wrapping up for Acme Casualty involving a kite surfer who claims a disabling back injury from a car crash but he still kites like a champion. I have photos from Keʻehi Lagoon to prove it.

Tommy shrugs.

Then I tell him about the Kauaʻi case I just turned down. That gets his attention. Tommy says he's had dealings with the Garden Isle attorney running for County Prosecutor, Janson Newfield. I tell him Mrs. Reece mentioned Newfield as a reason for her return to the islands to continue tracking the Barking Sands Strangler. Tommy remembers the murders of the three young women twenty years ago.

"How could you say no to that longsuffering mother, Kai?"

"I've learned the hard way. Disappoint 'em a little now rather than a lot later."

"If you change your mind, I can hook you up with Newfield. Although he must be busy now campaigning. But, I'll warn you, he's not my kind of guy. The man can't take a joke."

"*Oh . . .*" I say, as if I'm surprised. Tommy has a problem with conventional, straight-laced people in social situations. The problem is his off-color jokes.

"Well, Newfield's not taking a joke isn't the only reason," Tommy says as our sweet-and-sour spareribs arrive. "But since you passed on the case, no sense elaborating."

I pick up a rib, breathe in its lip-smacking aroma, and offer one to Tommy. He glances at the plate and shrugs.

"Not hungry?" I study his pallid face.

"Yeah, I'll take one." He reaches for the smallest rib and then munches on it tentatively.

"You sure you're okay?"

He nods and waves me off—shorthand for: We've exhausted the topic.

I move on. "The Barking Sands case would have been a bust. Besides, I'm keeping the decks clear for that big case you referred. T'anks, eh?"

"No problem," Tommy replies. "Any case for Matt Ossendorfer and his firm is a case worth waiting for."

"Can you tell me more about the Ossendorfer case?"

"You know already it involves a Detroit auto manufacturer and an accident on Maui." Tommy sets down his rib, hardly touched. "A car flipped near Makawao and the driver was ejected through the open sunroof and ended up paralyzed. The suit claims it was the car's fault. But the driver was intoxicated, has DUI arrests, and wasn't wearing a seat belt."

"That should be a slam-dunk."

"You'd think so," Tommy says, "but wheel a paralyzed plaintiff into the courtroom and the jury becomes sympathetic.

Ambulance-chasing attorneys know how to play the sympathy card. That's how they make their money. Ossendorfer doesn't want to take any chances. You'd be investigating on Maui, of course. Doing your usual stuff. Checking into the driver, his history, his family, and interviewing witnesses and people who know the injured man."

Our lemon chicken arrives and this time Tommy helps himself first—so I don't question him again about his health?—then passes it to me. I heap some of the steaming sweet citrus goodness onto my plate. Tommy starts slowly working on his chicken as I ask, "Any chance the plaintiff will settle out of court?"

"I don't think so. Potentially bigger money by going to trial."

"So, it's a go?" I ask because an out-of-court settlement might mean no case for me.

"Matt says it's just a question of when Detroit gives him the go ahead. He's not expecting any delays."

"Great. I'm wrapping up that insurance case—you know, the bogus victim who kite surfs like an Olympian with a girlfriend half his age. He's married with children, by the way."

I look up and here comes our pork fried rice. I love how in Chinese restaurants they bring out each dish at a different time. You never know what dish or when. It's always a surprise. I help myself and pass the rice to Tommy.

"Oh, yeah," he says, "you told me about that one. Did you nail him?"

"I snapped some photos that should carry the day in court."

Tommy looks around and changes the subject. "Where's

Viv tonight?" He's referring to my girlfriend, Vivienne Duvane. "You're not solo much anymore since you moved in with her."

"Viv teaches a class tonight."

"On Halloween?"

"Yup. Rain or shine."

"Are you still renting your apartment at the Waikīkī Edgewater?" Tommy picks up a few grains of fried rice with his chopsticks.

"Yeah. But I'm not sure how long I'll keep the bachelor pad. Doesn't make sense when I'm hardly ever there." I help myself to more lemon chicken.

"Unless things go south with Vivienne." Tommy raises his brows. "Like they did with Maile. And Nikki. And what was the name of that neurotic wife of the hotel tycoon?"

"Madison. Please don't remind me." I'm irked that Tommy would bring up my checkered history with women. "Vivienne's different. She slipped through my fingers once. She won't again."

Tommy smirks. "Am I hearing wedding bells?"

"I'm still a little gun shy," I say. "Viv left me the first time around for another guy—an academic like her."

"Ouch!" he grimaces.

"Tell me about it. Viv downplays her short-lived marriage to him and reassures me I'm her man, despite our differences."

"Some differences," Tommy says. "A college professor and a surfing gumshoe."

"That's what put her off before, I guess. But now she says we share a deeper connection than she ever did with him. Really irks me, though, that her ex- still calls her."

"I can see why," Tommy replies. "Does Viv want kids?"

I shrug. "We haven't discussed it. Besides we're both too busy for children. I wouldn't know how to parent anyway. My folks died when I was just a kid myself."

"Nevah know, brah. You might be a good father. You're dependable, steady, and caring . . . usually."

"Enough about my love life. How about you, Tommy?" He's had his own troubled relationships. Lately he's been dating a torch singer who works with his trio.

"What do I know about women?" Tommy admits. "I have enough trouble keeping my two cats."

"At least Miles and Charlie haven't walked out on you." I don't need to add—*like your two wives.*

Tommy turns even more pale.

"Sorry. Guess I'm a little touchy about Viv." I look down. "Just a bad joke."

Tommy perks up. "Speaking of jokes and wives, how do you know if your wife is a good housekeeper?"

I shake my head.

"After the divorce," Tommy manages a faint smile, "she keeps the house."

"Hmmm." I think for a moment about Vivienne's divorce. She did in fact keep the house. But hers was a different story. Entirely.

Before long we're finishing up with more hot tea. The check comes and we split it. Tommy slowly rises, then turns back and says, "Give the Barking Sands case a little more thought, Kai. I really feel for that mother."

"What about Ossendorfer? You said to keep the decks clear."

"That was before you told me about Mrs. Reece."

"So long, Tommy," I say, feeling another tug of conscience. "Get yourself checked by a doc."

three

Friday after Halloween I'm back on Maunakea Street waiting on the Ossendorfer case and fending off thoughts of Mrs. Reece. By mid-afternoon I head to Vivienne's place.

She lives in a quiet Kailua neighborhood of coco palms and putting-green lawns two blocks from the beach. A rambling ranch-style home in a shady cul-de-sac, her yard is large by Oʻahu standards and so is her swimming pool. She did well in her divorce. Recalling Tommy's joke, she's a good housekeeper. But Viv's case was hardly typical. Her husband went through a sea change that left her marooned, not to mention doubting herself. She deserved more from their marriage. More than a house.

I pull into her palm-lined driveway, deducing from the empty carport that Viv isn't home yet. I step from my car to the gregarious bark of a retriever. Kula—*gold* in Hawaiian—rushes out as soon as I crack the door. He gallops onto the front lawn with the grace of a stallion, his golden coat glowing in the sun.

"Hey boy!" I give him a hug. *"Walk?"*

He gets squirrely. He rolls on the grass. Then he dashes

into the house and returns in seconds with his leash clenched in his pearly white teeth.

We trot down to Kailua Beach and do our usual routine. I toss a fluorescent-yellow tennis ball into the waves and the golden boy plows in after it. Kula is a famous surfing dog—well, he's semi-retired now—who was stolen from a former client, a shady operator as it turned out. Pet detective Maile Barnes and I recovered the retriever, but instead of returning to his master Kula ended up with me. *Go figure.* How it happened still makes me shake my head. But you'd never guess such a fabulous dog could come from such a sordid crook.

I throw the yellow ball for Kula until my arm throbs. He's soaked and sandy and stoked. And he doesn't want to stop. I finally wade in after him and attach his leash.

Once we're home I rinse off his coat and we hang out on the *lānai* until Viv arrives around sunset. She pulls into the carport and emerges with a load of French books under an arm. I feel a familiar flutter inside as the willowy redhead glides toward me in a tropical-print dress that does wonders for her hazel eyes. Viv has just turned forty but could pass for one of her students. Gazing at her lithe and lovely figure, my old hurt fades away.

"Let me give you a hand with those books," I say as she reaches the *lānai*.

"Hello darlings," she says in her silvery tones. "How are my two favorite guys?" She hugs the retriever and gives me a kiss, her jasmine scent sending a shiver up my spine.

Vivienne, Kula and I step into her house. A cool breeze follows us in through open jalousies and wafts over the island furnishings and bamboo floors. Viv makes a beeline for the bathroom. Kula strides into the cozy den, circles his tartan plaid bed, and then deposits himself around stuffed animals, chews, and a doggie door leading to the swimming pool. *Rough life.* I plant myself in a rattan chair next to him. When Vivienne returns from the bathroom her face looks flushed.

"Feeling okay?" I ask.

"I may have a little fever," she replies. "And a I feel a bit queasy."

"Should you see a doctor?" I'm concerned, especially after the way Tommy cavalierly brushed off his symptoms.

She changes the subject. "How was your day?"

I tell her about my reluctantly refusing the Barking Sands case.

Vivienne is troubled by my turning away Mrs. Reece. "She lost her only child, Kai." Her voice rises. "And you *refused* her?"

"I thought you'd be proud of me," I reply, "for saying no to a fruitless case."

"Fruitless or not, this woman has endured the worst thing that can happen to a mother. How could you not feel that?"

"I *do* feel it. I just didn't think I could turn up anything new."

"Maybe you should reconsider." She utters this as a statement, not as a question.

"I can't afford to pass on Matt Ossendorfer." I tell her about the pending Detroit case referred by Tommy.

"You don't have to pass on Ossendorfer, whoever he is," Viv says. "You could comfort this poor woman just by telling her you'll take her case. She's waited twenty years. What do a few more weeks matter?"

There's no point in trying to explain to Vivienne at

this velvet hour about the challenges of a cold case twenty years old. And I don't want to anger her. I've learned from experience. So I simply say, "I'll think it over."

And over the weekend I do.

Sunday morning Vivienne and I are sitting on the *lānai* with Kula, sipping Kona coffee and reading the Honolulu paper. Viv is still not feeling quite right. She excuses herself to use the bathroom and is gone several minutes. She returns with a bewildered look.

"What's wrong?" I'm worried because she's so seldom ill.

She points to the bathroom.

I go have a look. Everything inside the bathroom appears normal. Towels neatly hung. Floor mat spotlessly clean in front of the sink. On the counter I notice something different—a little pink box labeled PREGNANCY TEST KIT. Sitting on top of the box is a lab test strip that says: ONE PINK LINE = NOT PREGNANT; TWO PINK LINES = PREGNANT. The strip shows two pink lines.

I carry it back to the *lānai*. "Is there something you want to tell me?"

"I'm not sure I did it right," she says. "What does it say?"

"It says you're pregnant."

"The kit is old," she says, "back when you and I first got together. Old kits sometimes give false positives."

"You should see a doctor. The sooner the better."

"I don't know. I never thought—especially at my age."

"You're barely forty," I say. "And you look twenty."

"That's why I love you." She flashes a heartbreaking smile.

"I'll help you make the appointment."

"I can do it," she says.

"First thing Monday morning?"

"Okay." She takes my hand.

At a moment like this you'd think we'd talk about what just happened. Instead, we keep sipping our coffee and reading the Sunday paper. It would be hard to put into words what I'm feeling. And Viv may be more at sea than I am. Before long she turns to me, not to talk about the pregnancy test but to show me a headline from Kaua'i.

GARDEN ISLE PROSECUTOR CANDIDATE'S DAUGHTER MISSING

The story says that Janson Newfield's daughter Alana disappeared Halloween night and has not been heard from since. Alana Newfield last appeared in a surveillance video leaving a Princeville hotel. A photo shows the stunning twenty-year-old and an accompanying campaign pic of her father.

"She must take after her mother," I say.

Viv nods. "The girl looks sweet and gorgeous. Her father looks, well, tough."

"Newfield's ads for county prosecutor no doubt harden his image for his law-and-order platform."

"That could explain it."

"Newfield promises to clean up the Garden Isle and to solve several cold cases," I explain, "including the Barking Sands murders. But that wasn't enough for Mrs. Reece. She wanted private boots on the ground."

"Do you think the girl's disappearance could be related to

her father's campaign?"

"I don't know. But with the election only days away, her going missing should focus attention on him."

"I hope she only wandered off." Viv looks concerned. "I hope, for her mother's sake, she only wandered off."

My cell phone rings. An unfamiliar number. Area code: 719. I let the call go to voicemail.

Within a minute my phone chimes indicating a new message.

"Did you see this morning's paper, Kai?" I recognize the caller's urgent voice. *Mrs. Reece.* "I'm worried about Alana Newfield. Just like I was worried about my Jenny twenty years ago. Would you please reconsider?"

When the voicemail ends Vivienne is curious, so I let her listen. She hands the phone back and just looks at me. Her glaring eyes say more than words.

That does it. The two people I trust most, Tommy and Vivienne, both agree. Not to mention Viv's startling news. I recall Mrs. Reece heartfelt words about parenthood—there's no love like the love for one's own child. Jennifer, she said, was the best thing that ever happened to her. And losing Jennifer was the worst.

I return Mrs. Reece's call and offer to take her case.

"I knew I could count on you." She sounds relieved. "I could see it in your eyes, even while you were saying no."

What do I telegraph to prospective clients that makes them think I'm the champion of lost causes and dead-end cases? I wish I knew. I've helped more than my share of penniless clients and gotten sucked into some unprofitable, not to mention dangerous, cases. I could blame it on my father's missionary ancestry and my adopted family's Hawaiian *aloha*. Maybe that's why I lend a hand when, if I were strictly business, I probably wouldn't.

"I have sympathy for any family whose child disappears," Mrs. Reece continues, "especially on the island where the Strangler once roamed. And may still."

"Do you have contacts on Kaua'i who knew Jennifer? And maybe others you've worked with on her case over the years?"

"Jen's surfing buddy, Ronnie—well, he was more than a buddy—would be glad to help, I'm sure. He never got over her. I met him only after Jennifer died, but I became fond of Ronnie and wished he and Jenny would have gotten together. Soon after she died he married on the rebound—unhappily."

"Has anyone in the Kaua'i Police Department worked with you?"

"Several officers. Most who were there when it happened have retired by now." She gives me names of a few officers she thinks are still on the force.

Then I ask a harder question: "Short of finding the Strangler himself, what would make my investigation successful in your eyes?"

"Turning up anything new we can build on to eventually find him."

Though her expectations sound more realistic than I expected, I'm convinced what she really wants from me is nothing less than to fulfill her life's mission. So I simply say, "I'll do my best."

Before we wrap up, I explain to Mrs. Reece my standard contract. I tell her she can sign and submit a retainer in my office on Monday.

After the call Vivienne congratulates me for what she says is my doing the right thing and then we go back to the Sunday paper. We read silently. Neither of us seems to know how to start a conversation about the pregnancy test.

four

On Monday Vivienne calls Kapiolani Medical Center for Women and Children and arranges an appointment for that afternoon. I head to Maunakea Street to meet with Mrs. Reece.

We take care of business and then I drive down King Street past the only royal residence in America to the Hawai'i State Library. Though not as majestic as Iolani Palace, the library funded by Andrew Carnegie dates back a hundred years and boasts Tuscan columns, Palladian arched windows, and flowering monkeypod trees on the rambling green corner of Punchbowl and King. The state library is a comfy place to curl up in its cool alcoves with a book. Or to dig into local newspaper files on one of the islands' most notorious serial killers.

I make my way to the Hawai'i Room. I could search the internet from my office, but the collections here go much deeper and carry both Honolulu dailies and the Kaua'i newspaper, *The Garden Island,* from the era of the murders. I want to find out more about the Strangler's MO and his victims before I hop a plane to my favorite neighbor island.

Here's what I find: Three young women—Jennifer Reece,

Tara Marie Havens, and Elise Morneau—went missing a few weeks apart one summer two decades ago. Jennifer, my client's daughter, vanished from Polihale State Park, a wild and remote beach on Kaua'i's West Side. The chestnut-haired, green-eyed beauty was the first victim and her abduction by an unknown man who shuffled up from nearby Barking Sands Beach gave the Strangler his name. Jennifer's remains were later discovered in Waimea Canyon, about twenty miles distant from Polihale, with the telltale signature of the Strangler—a crude wave tattooed with thirteen cigarette burns.

The second and youngest victim, the raven-haired Tara Marie Havens, nineteen, disappeared one night a few weeks later from Līhu'e, probably near Kaua'i Community College where she was a student. No witnesses to her abduction had ever come forward. Tara's remains, like Jennifer's, were found in Waimea Canyon and she bore the same crude wave. The third and only married victim, Elise Morneau, twenty-four, was a nurse at a women's clinic near Hanapepe. The blonde RN went missing one evening later that summer while riding her bicycle to meet a friend for dinner. Elise's remains, as those of the other two victims, were discovered in the canyon with the same signature.

It's not hard to find similarities in the three murders. All victims were attractive young Caucasian women in their late teens and early twenties—one a surfer, one a student, and one a nurse. The first (Jennifer Reece) disappeared in broad daylight, the other two in evening hours. All three women's remains showed signs of strangulation: burst blood vessels in the eyes and eyelids, faces indicating suffocation, along with heavy bruises on their throats forming a dark band around their necks. Physical evidence was degraded, decomposition hampering but not defeating efforts to recover tissue and bodily fluids that could be matched to suspects by DNA.

What else did the victims have in common? Two were alone when they encountered the Strangler, while Jennifer was on an isolated but not deserted beach. He was seen, at a distance, luring her into a parking lot from which she disappeared with no witnesses.

Kaua'i Police compiled a list of persons of interest in the serial murders. A convicted rapist on parole at the time named Theron Walter appeared to be the prime suspect until DNA tests proved inconclusive. Many on the Garden Isle believed Walter was the guy. But he got away. Well, not exactly. He went back to prison on a parole violation but was never charged in the Barking Sands murders.

What did the Strangler look like? The very few witnesses said no features stood out. Dark hair, maybe dark brown. He often wore sunglasses. He sometimes hobbled and looked disabled. He was above medium height and good looking. He apparently did not frighten the young women. Just the opposite. He got them to cooperate with him and to help him. His ability to win over victims, to make them feel safe, may be the same ability that allowed him to hide in plain sight, living a double life: respectable citizen one day, serial killer the next.

Back in my office later that day I check active cold cases on the Kaua'i County Prosecutor's Office website. I find all three women murdered by the Strangler twenty years ago. And also Amity Johnson, found dead ten years later. Then I search my trusted database for background on the victims and their families. I also search other individuals associated with them. Anyone who knew the victims could be a potential source of new information, even if they had been interviewed at the time of the murders.

Then I check missing people on Kaua'i. Alana Newfield appears first on the list. She was last seen Halloween night leaving a Princeville hotel. I do a background check on Alana and find something surprising. She has an arrest record in Seattle. Alana was attending Saint Ursula College, a religious women's institution, when she got busted. The nature of the offense is not clear from the coding in the database. For that, I will have to dig deeper.

Why would the daughter of a man campaigning for Kaua'i County Prosecutor find herself at odds with the law? There may be a simple explanation. A protest rally? A sit-in? Or some other matter of social conscience or political action that pitted a college student against the establishment? Since Alana is a missing person and a side issue to my cold-case murder investigation at this point, I let it go for now.

Then I make some calls to set up interviews on Kaua'i. I start with Jennifer Reece's former surfing buddy, Ronnie, who agrees to drive with me to Polihale State Park. Ronnie seems more than willing to help and adamantly refuses compensation for his time. He appears to relish talking about Jen, as he calls her, even twenty years after her horrific death. She was apparently the love of his life—the love that never flowered but could never be equaled. Ronnie has contacts with surviving friends and family of the other two victims. He says people close to the victims bonded back then. He's still in touch with some of them. He gives me two names. Dawn

Lee, RN, director of the clinic in Ele'ele near Hanapepe where Elise Morneau was a nurse and Dr. Gwen Kalama, Vice Chancellor at Kaua'i Community College, who knew student Tara Marie Havens.

Since I doubt I'll get much if any cooperation on my own from the Kaua'i Police Department, I turn to my old buddy in Homicide on the Honolulu force. I haven't spoken much with Frank Fernandez since the big man married Maile. To say we're old buddies would be a stretch, actually. We've never been what you might call close. But we've occasionally worked together and helped each other out. Sometimes we disagree. Well, we often disagree. I give him a call.

"Howzit, Frank?" I ask, feeling lucky to catch him in.

"Kind of busy, Kai." His deep, gravelly impatient voice might scare away someone who hasn't known him as long as I have.

"Only take a minute," I reply.

"Good, 'cause I've hardly got a minute."

"Frank, you know anybody on the Kaua'i force?"

"I do. What's it to you?" Is Frank in one of his notorious foul moods?

"I'm working a longshot cold case on the Garden Isle and I need some help. You remember the Barking Sands Strangler?"

"Course I do." More impatience.

"I'm looking for him."

"You're *what?*"

"I'm looking for the Strangler. I tried in every way I know to nix the case, but I got it anyway."

"Why didn't you just say no?"

"I did. Three or four times."

He puffs into the phone like he can't believe it.

"Look, Frank, my client is a mother who lost her only child to the Strangler and she's never stopped searching for him, after twenty years."

"Touching," he says, sounding half sarcastic and half sympathetic. "So how can I help you?" Maybe he really does feel sympathy?

"Nobody at KPD is going to give me the time of day, Frank. They don't want a PI from a neighbor island nosing around in an old case they never solved."

"You got that one right," he says. "In the unlikely event you find anything, you make them look bad."

"There's no point in my walking into Kaua'i Police headquarters on my own—with no contact on the inside—with no referral."

"Uh-huh," he mumbles.

"So, Frank, do you know anybody on the Garden Isle force who would at least talk to me?"

"Try Nakamura," he says without a moment's thought.

"Who's he?"

"*She,*" Frank replies. "Ellen Nakamura, a detective who works cold cases in Investigative Services."

"Okay if I drop your name?"

"Go ahead. But you owe me one." He rattles off her phone number.

"I always pay you back, don't I, Frank?"

"I s'pose," he says half-heartedly.

"T'anks, eh?"

"Good luck, Kai." He grunts. "You'll need it."

I punch in the number Frank gave me and get the

detective's voicemail. I drop Fernandez' name and explain I'll be on Kauaʻi the next day and would appreciate speaking with her about the Barking Sands case. I leave my number but don't expect she'll return my call. I only hope that tomorrow when I knock on her door she'll open it.

Later that afternoon I drive to Kapiolani Medical Center for Women and Children. I ask directions to the OB-GYN department. I step into the waiting room and fortunately Vivienne is still sitting patiently before her appointment.

"Darling!" She's surprised to see me. "What are you doing here?"

"Wouldn't miss this for the world."

"I like it," she says. "I like that we'll be together when we find out."

Her turn comes and they take her into an examining room. I'm permitted to accompany her. A nurse gives Viv a clear plastic cup. My eyes follow her as she steps to a restroom down the hall. I'm feeling like my life is suddenly about to change—*forever*. I recall Mrs. Reece asking me if I had children and then my responding to her in a flip way that implied an affirmative answer would have been unthinkable. *Maybe not?* I'm lucky, at least, that I couldn't be more confident in the mother of this potential child.

Vivienne is one of those exceptional women who has it all. Brains and beauty. Heart. Passion. Strength. Integrity. Whether she's in the classroom inspiring her students or in the street waving signs for her causes, it's the same Vivienne. She's genuine through and through. She's had her problems and disappointments in life. Haven't we all? But every cloud, as they say, has a silver lining. What she once considered her gravest failure, her divorce, brought us back together. I've forgiven her for not trusting what we had the first time around, despite the heartache it caused. Who could blame her? A gumshoe surfer and a professor of French, as Tommy observed, hardly seemed a likely match.

"How did it go?" I ask Vivienne when she returns from the restroom.

"No big deal. I peed into the cup."

We wait in the examination room several minutes. Eventually a doctor in a white coat waltzes in with the verdict. Positive. Vivienne's face flushes. She takes a deep breath.

The doctor notices. She puts her hand on the expectant mother's shoulder. "We'll be with you all the way," she reassures Viv.

Some particulars are discussed and another appointment is arranged.

"Are you happy?" I ask her when the doctor departs.

"I'm delirious. I never thought—" she says, the color remaining in her face. "How do you feel?"

"I never doubted the home pregnancy test."

"But how do you *feel?*"

"Uh," I grapple for words. "It's kind of a rush—like riding the wave of my life."

"Good. Let's start thinking of baby names."

"Already?"

"It may take a while and we need names for both a boy and a girl."

"Later, we'll find out which one?"

"If we want to. Is that important to you?"

"I was just wondering."

"I love you," she says. "And we're going to have a baby."

"I love you too." I've rarely said this to anyone since my parents died. For Viv I make an exception.

I take her hand and we step into our uncharted future.

five

Tuesday, Election Day, I fly to Kaua'i. One of the shortest routes in commercial aviation—about twenty minutes in the air—the taxi out from Honolulu Airport and taxi in to Līhu'e Airport can take as long as the flight itself. It's a quick trip. Not even much time to think. But I do—about Vivienne and the baby.

What the short flight to Kaua'i lacks in duration it makes up in visual splendor. As the airplane descends over lush fairways and coconut palms and emerald lagoons, that first glimpse of the Garden Isle always takes my breath away. Several places on earth wear the moniker of tropical paradise, but few places deliver like Kaua'i. If you're looking for dazzling sunshine, balmy air, caressing breezes, gentle rains, and eye-popping beauty get your ticket stamped to this lovely little island.

In such a beautiful place who would expect serial murder?

After we touch down I rent a Jeep Wrangler and head for Kaua'i Police Department headquarters. A radio news report says polls show Janson Newfield holding a narrow lead in the race for County Prosecutor over the incumbent Buddy Kalaheo. If Newfield's poll results hold after all votes are cast and counted, sometime late tonight or early tomorrow morning Kaua'i will have a new prosecutor. I hope that will prove good news for Mrs. Reece.

KPD headquarters is less than half a mile from Līhu'e Airport. It's a no-brainer to stop there first, since from the car rental agency I spot its green tile roof over treetops. Election day in the islands is a state, county, and city holiday, but police departments never close.

The institutional beige building housing Garden Isle law enforcement and the county prosecutor could pass for a low-security prison. Concrete lattice covering windows gives it a fortified look. Green lawns and ornamental palms soften the penal effect. In fact, temporary holding cells occupy an important part of the facility.

As I climb the outdoor stairs to the second floor I try to imagine the atmosphere inside the county prosecutor's office on Election Day when the incumbent is behind in the polls. I'll never know because I'm heading across the hall to the Office of Investigative Services. Both offices are secured behind thick plate glass. I step to the investigative side and speak into an intercom. I explain that I was referred by HPD Detective Frank Fernandez and left a message yesterday for Detective Nakamura. There's a long pause. I feel an emptiness in the pit of my stomach. Then I hear a buzz and the receptionist tells me to push open the glass door.

It's a quiet morning inside Investigative Services—only a few personnel in sight. I ask for the detective and am ushered into an inner office where a female officer is talking to a male patrol sergeant.

Nakamura is a trim and fit woman in her mid-thirties with

an open smile, shiny brown hair pulled back into a bun, and luminous brown eyes. She wears a wedding ring and, from the conversation I overhear, her throaty voice conveys authority.

She looks at me and says, "So, your buddy Fernandez sent you?"

"Not my buddy exactly." I hand her my Surfing Detective card. "But I've known him for years."

"I hear ya." Nakamura scans the wave-rider card. "Frank can be a teddy bear—"

"If you catch him on a good day," I finish her thought.

She laughs. "Oh." The detective turns to her fellow officer. "Kai, this is Sergeant Zhao, West Side patrol officer. We were just discussing an unsolved case in Kekaha."

"Howzit, Kai."

"Howzit, Sergeant Zhao? Don't let me interrupt."

"The sergeant and I were just finishing up," Nakamura says and Zhao departs.

I watch him leave and take note that the culture of the Kaua'i Police Department must have changed since the serial murders twenty years ago, when the force was predominantly male. A woman detective back then would have been rare. That doesn't mean I'll get any more cooperation from her than I would from a male officer.

Nakamura is cordial and friendly and speaks in generalities about the Strangler cases. She even apologizes that she can't tell me more. It is what it is.

"Look, Kai, we've put every available resource on these cold cases," she reassures me. "I wish those resources sometimes could have been more, but we're a small department."

"I understand," I say. "I only took this case because the

mother of one of the victims pleaded with me."

"Oh, you mean Marian Reece—Jennifer's mother?"

"You know her?"

"Of all the victims' families, Marian has been the most persistent in keeping us on the case. And I guarantee you we have been on the case to the extent we can."

I ask about a Strangler suspect. "Could you tell me about Theron Walter? He was on the top of your list, right? And he walked?"

"That was before my time. I was barely a teenager back then. But I can tell you Walter didn't exactly walk. He's still in prison for sexual assault. He claimed he was having consensual sex on the beach with a woman who didn't agree."

"He was out when all three murders happened?"

"Yes, he was. DNA evidence was inconclusive, and no eyewitness could positively identify him."

"Doesn't mean he's not the guy."

"No, but we still have others on the list—a half dozen."

"That list would be interesting to see."

"I'd share it with you, Kai, but if I got caught I'd be back on the late show. Night patrol is tough when you have kids at home."

"Understood. You don't want to lose your job in Investigative Services."

Detective Nakamura checks her watch. I take the hint and turn toward the door. Though I've got nothing from her but chit-chat, I say, "Mahalo for seeing me."

"In the unlikely event you find anything we didn't, you'll let us know?" She hands me her own card. "We want this guy as much as you do."

"For sure." I make my way to the door.

"Wait, Kai." She follows me. "Let me walk you out."

We pass through the thick glass door together into the open-air mezzanine across from the prosecutor's office. We're alone.

"Try Ernie Hong," she says almost in a whisper.

"Who?" I ask.

"Ernie's a retired KPD officer who was on the force during the Barking Sands investigation. He lives in Kōloa." She rattles off his phone number.

"Thanks." I quickly put Ernie Hong's number in my phone contacts.

Detective Nakamura turns toward her office, then back to me and says: "Ernie may be able to help you where I couldn't."

Climbing into my rental Jeep a few minutes later I give retired Detective Ernie Hong a call. I'm heading to the town of Waimea on the West Side, but Kōloa is not much out of the way. Hong answers, he's home, and he can see me now. In fact, it's as if he were expecting my call.

Did Nakamura have this planned all along? Is she secretly hoping to get any help she can on these very cold cases? I don't know. But it does seem like I'm receiving more cooperation—indirectly—than I expected.

I take Kaumuali'i Highway from Līhu'e southwest toward the sunny beaches of Po'ipū. At Knudsen Gap where the hillside route threads narrowly between two razorback ridges I turn onto Maluhia Road and shoot due south through the famous mile-long stretch of giant eucalyptus called the Tree Tunnel. Their gnarly trunks look ravaged by hurricanes and time, but their boughs still reach over the highway, forming a nearly unbroken green canopy.

I stop a few miles short of those sunny beaches at old Kōloa town, home of the first sugar plantation in the Hawaiian Islands. Driving by Kōloa's folksy red clapboard buildings I'm reminded of sleepy Kaunakakai on Moloka'i, where past investigations have taken me and where the pace of life slows to the heartbeat of the people.

The home of retired Kaua'i Police Detective Ernie Hong is about a quarter mile further off Waikomo Road. I aim up his earthen driveway to a cozy cottage surrounded by tropical plants and lily pads floating in a koi pond. The abundance of growing things suggests somebody here has a green thumb.

Before long a statuesque man steps out. Despite his surname, Hong looks as much Hawaiian as Chinese, with burnished brown skin and wavy silver hair. And he also looks familiar. I can't recollect ever meeting him before. Why do I feel like I know him?

I step from my car and shake his hand. "Ernie, thanks for seeing me on short notice. I'm Kai Cooke."

"Aloha, Kai."

"Have we met before?" I study his pleasant face. He is, as they say, easy on the eyes.

"I get that all the time," Ernie says. "TV commercials for local banks, insurance companies, and grocery chains."

"That's it!" I remember now seeing him on the small screen. Ernie was that archetypal good-looking local man that you could always trust.

"Was my second job besides the force. On days off I'd do shoots here on Kaua'i and sometimes on the other islands."

"Must have been fun?" I ask.

"Not the commercials, so much," Ernie replies, "but way back I landed a bit part on the old *Hawaii Five-0*. 'Book 'em, Danno,' you know?"

"Cool!" I'm impressed.

"I played myself. A cop." Ernie sighs. "Not many roles or commercials for me anymore. Only when they need a grandpa."

Ernie leads me to a *lānai* bordered by red ti plants and overlooking his koi pond. We sit by a small round table and he rises and then returns with two bottles of beer.

"Mahalo!" I take a swig. I don't usually drink on the job, but I can't refuse the hospitality of my host. Plus, the cold beer tastes good.

"Ellen told me you were coming," Ernie says, referring to Detective Nakamura. "Nice lady. And *akamai*—smart, you know? Was no *wahine* on the force like her back in my day." He sighs.

"Detective Nakamura couldn't tell me much about the Barking Sands Strangler case," I say, "but I hope you can."

"Tough case," Ernie explains. "So much pressure to find the killer. People on the island were scared. Especially *wahine*. And after a while they got impatient and upset with the department. We were doing everything we could. We interviewed dozens of registered sex offenders. And we brought in a few who were on parole. We scoured the island. But unlike on *Hawaii Five-0* we couldn't arrest the bad guy in one sixty-minute episode. Doesn't often happen that way in real police work."

"Why was it so tough?"

"There just wasn't much physical evidence. And by the

time the victims were found any footprints or tire tracks or other evidence had really deteriorated."

"How about DNA?"

"We got some DNA samples that we couldn't connect to anyone here locally or on the mainland through the FBI's database."

"Nothing, huh?"

Ernie nods. "Little evidence and few witnesses—none who could positively ID any suspect. Like I told you, it wasn't that we didn't try and keep trying. In the months that followed several guys were brought in for questioning. One even confessed."

"I never heard about a confession."

"It led nowhere. We soon realized he couldn't have done it and he didn't do it."

"Bummahs."

"Plenny more leads. But goin' nowhere."

"Didn't you have a list of suspects?"

"We cast our net wide, so our list was long and contained some guys who didn't even get a look. But about a half dozen stood out. They were on the top of our list. We believed then—and I still believe—the Strangler is among them."

I ask about the sex offender who was out on parole when the murders happened. "Is Theron Walter on top?"

Hong nods. "A few of us old-timers still like him for all three murders, but we never had a strong enough case. He wasn't charged. You'd think after twenty years we'd have something that would stand up in court."

"The detective mentioned that Theron Walter is back in prison."

"Yeah, he's on Oʻahu at Halawa."

I make a mental note to visit Walter when I return to Oʻahu. I ask, "Ernie, can you share the six on your list?"

"If I was still on the force, I couldn't. But I'm retired now, Kai. That's I guess why Ellen sent you. She wants to crack this cold case. She'll take help wherever she can."

"Unofficially?"

Ernie nods again, steps away, and returns with a half dozen sheets of paper. One by one his displays five mug shots and one police sketch: Stephen "Stubby" Kahale, Korgan Lew, Joel Merryweather, Michael Julio Rabino, Theron Walter, and the sketch of a man with nondescript regular features and dark hair. I already know now the whereabouts of two on the list. After incarceration for a rape conviction Korgan Lew is out on parole and back on the Garden Isle. Theron Walter, as Hong mentioned, is doing time again in Halawa prison.

"How did the sketch come about?"

"Like I told you, no witness could ID anyone we brought in, but a few described someone else we didn't. And to this day we have never found him."

"May I please snap pics of the six, Ernie?"

He nods and I do. Then I ask a follow-up question: "Do you have names for the others who didn't make top six on the list?"

"No, I didn't bother," he says. "They were all long shots."

"Do you remember anyone you were curious about but didn't pursue? Maybe who still lives on Kauaʻi?"

Ernie thinks for a moment. "There was one guy who lived on the West Side near where the first victim was abducted and not far from Waimea Canyon where all the bodies were gs started on the West Side at Polihale

d then Līhuʻe suggested that the killer

Side and work in Līhuʻe, and travel

those two points. But no suspect was investigated
that followed that pattern."

"Anything else?"

"I remember he worked for the county in some capacity
and had no record."

"Where does he live on the West Side?" I ask, knowing
from experience that small towns there like Waimea and
Kekaha are not far from Polihale.

"Can't remember." Hong apologizes. "Like I said, he was
a longshot."

six

I thank Ernie Hong and then drive to where the crimes began on the West Side. Passing through Kalaheo, Eleʻele, and Hanapepe I wonder how a rapist and murderer of three women escapes detection for two decades. When major crimes like these are committed law enforcement may receive a flood of tips, far too many for their stretched resources to investigate. Decisions must be made as to which tips could lead to an arrest and conviction. Persons low on the list sometimes get passed over. How about all those low-list names? Ernie Hong remembered one on the West Side. I'd still like to see that entire list.

The two main attractions on the West Side—seventeen miles of sandy beaches from Waimea town to Polihale State Park and majestic Waimea Canyon—are also main crime scenes in the case. Jennifer Reece was abducted from Polihale and her body was recovered in the canyon.

After a dozen more miles on Kaumualiʻi Highway I arrive in the town of Waimea where I'm to meet Jennifer's former surfing buddy—whose love for her blossomed too late. Even in November it's hot. Though Kauaʻi is known for rain, its

West Side gets little. And often records the Garden Isle's highest daily temperatures. Trade winds and their showers— typically blowing east to west—usually weaken by the time they get here, leaving the land arid and dusty red. Except when the Kona winds kick in from the opposite direction, you can usually count on the West Side being dry and sunny. No surprise its beaches would attract a surfer like Jennifer Reece.

I pick up Ronnie at an open-air eatery along the highway called the Shrimp Shack. He's standing by the curb—shaved "bolo" head, brooding eyes, and beefy shoulders—his bronzed hard body reminding me of surfing ironman Kelly Slater. Ronnie must be in his mid-forties but looks as fit as a much younger man.

He jumps in.

"Thanks for showing up." I extend my hand. "I'm Kai."

"Anything I can do for Jen's mom." Ronnie applies his steel grip, his deep voice echoing his surfer brawn. "No one should suffer like Mrs. Reece. She's been alone in the world so many years. But she's never stopped looking for the Strangler."

"I'm on the case, Ronnie." I pull away from the Shrimp Shack. "Maybe you can help?"

"I'll try. Jen was the best ever." His big voice quiets and fragility suddenly shows in his ironman face. "I still miss her."

We head down the highway past the Pacific Missile Range, best known for its interceptor rockets of President Reagan's Star Wars campaign. There's not much to see of the secured facility from the road. Clusters of low buildings line a runway along shore, surrounded by chain link and barbed wire. Sentry posts stand at entry points. Back in the day when Jennifer was murdered, access to Barking Sands and other West Side beaches was open through the base. Then came September 11, 2001. Everything changed. Gates slammed shut. Beach access has been severely restricted ever since. Polihale State Park, north of the Range, fortunately has remained open, but getting there has never been a picnic, even before 9/11.

Ronnie breaks the silence. "It still makes me angry that Jen was ripped from me by that guy. I'm dreading going back."

"Thanks again, man," I say as we come to the end of the paved road. "It can't be easy for you."

He nods, unfolds one of his muscular arms, and points. "This is our turn. Get ready for a bumpy ride."

I hang a left into overgrown cane fields. The red dirt road snaking through them has potholes as big as bathtubs. No kidding. Suddenly we're rocking and rolling. It's a kidney-bruising ride—even in a Jeep. I take my foot off the accelerator and we idle along at little more than walking speed. But at least we don't lose our fillings. Even at this pace the Wrangler groans over the craters. It's like climbing swells in a gale at sea. I grip the steering wheel, trying to hold her steady over the caverns. The things I do for my clients.

"How long is this rocky ride?" I ask Ronnie.

"Five miles," he replies. "They say you can do it in thirty minutes, but only if you drive twice as fast as we're going."

"Twice as fast? And break an axle? Or an arm?"

He laughs.

"Was the road this bad twenty years ago when Jennifer disappeared?"

"Bad. But not this bad. Only when it rained."

"Then the Strangler could have made a quick getaway—

impossible today?"

"Right. Depending upon what kind of vehicle he drove."

We don't talk much after that. Ronnie looks straight ahead, lips tight. I feel bad dragging the big man back here. But I try to stay focused on the potholes.

After four very long miles the cratered road turns to sand. A good sign. But we've got another mile in the soft stuff. I'm glad all four wheels are pulling. Soon the sky ahead turns bright blue. The beach is coming. The Na Pali range soars into view, its purple peaks marking the southern edge of that famed wilderness unreachable except by boat or helicopter or hiking trails.

Before long we take another left into the sandy lot of Polihale State Park. I pull up to two other vehicles and several warning signs: HIGH SURF. DANGEROUS SHORE BREAK. STRONG CURRENT. We hop out. Feral chickens with bright red combs roam the lot and peck the sand.

"This is where Jen parked her car." Ronnie points to an empty space in the lot. "It was still here late afternoon after I searched the beach."

"Did the Strangler park here too?"

"Most likely."

"Any idea what his vehicle looked like?"

"Quite a few cars were here that day. Not like today. I couldn't tell you which was his. I wish I could." The ironman looks pained.

"No worries. No reason you'd be looking until you realized Jen was missing. By then, the Strangler would have been gone."

Before hiking the beach we use the sketchy public rest-

room. Dripping faucets. Overflowing rubbish bins. Missing
toilet seats. No wonder, considering the third-world road to
get here.

"Over this way," Ronnie says as we regroup by an outdoor
shower where a young woman and man in skimpy black
speedos—Europeans?—are rinsing off. We hike a winding
path up a shoreline dune, the brooding Na Pali ridgeline
casting its dark shadow behind us. We tramp over the *naupaka*-
festooned dune for our first glimpse of the beach. Caramel-
colored and as wide as a football field.

Nobody is in the water and for good reason. The surf is
wild. Double overhead. Closeout sets. And a wicked shore
break. Despite the gemlike turquoise hue of the offshore sea,
closer in is boiling soup. Not safe for even wading.

"A beginner or an expert can have fun here," Ronnie says.
"Quick peaks and hollow sections."

He must see my look of disbelief. "The rip currents alone
could take down an experienced waterman. And no reefs to
tame the surf. Would you really go out in this today?"

"I meant in the summer," he explains. "It's calmer then.
And busier."

"Hard to imagine." Nearly an empty beach today. A couple
of pup tents on the dunes. A decaying boogie board hanging
from a piece of driftwood. A fisherman casting his line halfway
to Nohili Point. Not a single surfer.

I gaze south where the wide beach stretches for miles past
the missile range to Kekaha, and the green dunes roll like an
epic wave down the coast. There's a raw wildness to this place
that makes it feel far from civilization. Some say this sandy
stretch is the westernmost point of the United States—the

end of the western world. Polihale does seem on the edge of something.

Ronnie gestures to a jutting peninsula to the south. "Barking Sands begins down at Nohili Point and runs up this way."

"That's where the Strangler came from?"

"Yeah, he was walking. Well, he was limping. Back then the beach was a favorite hangout of hippies and vagrants who camped on the dunes and picked shells at sunrise. The guy didn't look out of place. Nobody did back then."

"Jenny surfed here often?"

"She did. Polihale and Barking Sands were her favorites."

"Could you show me where you saw her on the beach that last time?"

"Let's do it, man!" Ronnie sounds like he wants to get it over with. He leads the way.

We tramp along in the sand. Beyond the surf, across the ocean, we can see the faint outline of the Forbidden Island, Ni'ihau.

"Jenny liked to keep her distance from the showers and all," Ronnie says as we continue hiking. "Fewer people."

"I don't like crowds either."

"Me too." Ronnie heads toward the tall dunes. He seems to know exactly where he's going. "It's been a long time, but the spot is seared in my mind."

"I hear ya," I say as we get closer. "What more can you tell me about her?"

"Jen was fun. And funny. She loved everyone, especially the autistic kids she worked with. And she was smart—straight As at Boulder. Jen had long, honey-colored hair and beautiful eyes. I always thought they were green. But the missing person report called them blue. Anyway, you should have seen her in a bikini." He slowly shakes his head. "I flipped for her right away, even though she was dating another guy."

We keep tramping, then Ronnie slows. "We're almost there."

We step to a break in the dunes where a sandy path cuts through.

"Here," he points to the empty sand. "She was sitting on her mat when the guy walked up."

"Walked or limped?"

"Limped, like I said before. At least, when he got close to Jen. He stopped to talk to her. Before long she was following him as he hobbled toward the lot where we parked today. She was carrying something for him, I assume."

"What did he look like?"

"He was taller than Jen. Not by much. He wore aviator sunglasses. Board shorts and a t-shirt. Dark hair. The two seemed to be talking animatedly—friendly-like."

"Did the guy resemble any of these?" I show Ronnie the six suspect photos on my phone.

Ronnie looks closely at each image and then apologizes. "Sorry, man. The guy was too far away. I couldn't make him out other than what I just told you."

"What about the guy Jen was dating?"

"Never met him. She said his name was Mitch. Nice manners. Had some college. Frankly, I think she was about to break up with Mitch. At least I hoped she was. And then—" Ronnie's deep voice cuts off. Soon he chokes out, "Too late."

I pat him on his meaty shoulder. "Sorry, man."

"My life might have turned out diff—" He stops again and turns away.

I give him a moment to get composed and then ask: "You never heard anything more about Mitch? I mean, after she was gone?"

"I told Kaua'i Police about him. But for all I know nothing came of it."

"Back to the Strangler. You didn't think anything of Jennifer helping this guy limping up from Barking Sands?"

"I saw nothing strange. Jennifer was like that. Sweet and generous. Quick to help others."

"And you didn't see her or him after that?"

"No. When I finished surfing I noticed her stuff on the beach—her towel and mat and coverup. Her surfboard was gone, so I figured she was in the water. I didn't spot her out there, but I hung around for a while waiting for her."

"How long did you wait?"

"Must have been close to an hour. It was late afternoon. When she didn't show up I got worried. I couldn't find her in the water or on the beach or in the lot. Her car was still there. I asked around. But nobody else had seen her either."

"Then you went for help?"

He nods. "I drove out the cane road to the first sentry post I came to at the missile range. The sentry called Kaua'i police. It took a while, but they eventually showed up. They searched the beach. Around sunset a helicopter flew in and cruised back and forth over the surf. The search went on until dark."

"They didn't find her surfboard?"

"Not then. Her board was recovered later. I don't know

where they found it or how. I think most people assumed she had drowned or was attacked by a shark. But with no body and nothing of hers left behind except her stuff on the beach, there was zero evidence of either. Then that missing person report I told you about was filed."

"They found her weeks later?"

"Yeah. Pig hunters in Waimea Canyon came across her body. Their dogs found her hidden in underbrush. I heard she was naked when they found her with a wave . . ." he hesitates, "burned on her bare breast."

I pat him again. "You still really miss her."

He closes his eyes, fighting back tears, and nods. "This is the last place I ever saw Jen."

"My bad for dragging you out here."

"Glad you did. I feel closer to her than I have in years."

"Some people I guess we never get over."

"Tell me about it. When Jen died I was reeling. I married too quickly. My ex-wife and I had a pair of boys before I figured it out. They're great kids. But their dad never got over his first love."

I shake my head. More collateral damage?

He pulls a photo from his wallet. It's that one Mrs. Reece showed me of Jennifer all smiles on a sunny beach wearing her silver locket. "I took this photo right here," Ronnie says, "only a few days after I first met her. I was already head-over-heels."

"The smile she's beaming back," I say, "tells me she was feeling something for you too."

"Think so?" He perks up.

"I do." I think I'm right but if not, what's the harm?

"I gave a copy to Jen's mother," he says. "And I have an enlargement framed at home. My wife didn't like seeing it. But after we divorced I brought it out again."

As we walk back to the lot I reflect on how it happened—how Jennifer Reece was abducted by an unknown man shambling up from Barking Sands Beach. I know a little more than I did before. But who that man was remains as much a mystery today as it was twenty years ago.

seven

From Polihale we double back to Kekaha and then head up Waimea Canyon Drive, twisting and turning toward the summit near Kokeʻe State Park. The remoteness of the canyon gave the Strangler something he desperately needed—safe haven to hide three bodies. Ronnie says he can show me where each was found.

As we climb we catch another glimpse of Niʻihau, its long shadowy flank resembling a humpback whale breaching the ocean's placid plane. The sparse vegetation of the arid West Side transforms along the ascending highway into the lusher ferns and mosses and flowering ʻohiʻa of the canyon rainforest.

Ronnie shows me where to pull off the highway. We hop out and hike up a narrow path into the gaping chasm formed by successive eruptions and lava flows. Waimea Canyon reveals its geological history in reddish strata on ridgelines resembling a many-layered mango cake. As we climb the air grows cooler and misty clouds drift skyward—evaporating into thin air. *Magical.*

As at Polihale, Ronnie knows right where to go. He leads us to a rock ridge and he says, "This is the spot."

I peer over the ridge that drops a couple hundred feet, easy. "Really?"

"Not down there," he explains. "Behind you." Ronnie points to a thicket of twisted *koa*.

Anybody hiking to this lookout would take in the view but not glance behind it at that tangle of trees. The Strangler was no dummy. He could have simply pushed his victims over the cliff, but he chose secluded burrows along the trail instead.

"In the hollow under these *koa* limbs," Ronnie says. "That's where they found her."

I scope out a little den hidden behind the camouflage of gnarly green. Just the right size for a body.

"Twenty years. The landscape has changed a little," he says matter-of-factly, "but this is the place." Jen's burial site doesn't seem to affect Ronnie like the beach where he last saw her alive.

"How did they find her?" I've read accounts but want to hear his version.

"Pig hunters. Their dogs went crazy when they came upon this spot. And then the hunters discovered Jen."

"Did you see her remains here yourself?" I know the answer but ask, hoping he'll remember more.

"No. Police removed her before I came up. I don't know what good I thought it would do. But I came anyway. I wanted to see her last resting place. If you can call it that."

"You weren't asked to identify her?"

Ronnie shakes his head. "No, like I said, last time I saw Jen was on the beach. Her mother, poor woman, flew in from Colorado to identify her. Why do you ask?"

"Oh, I was wondering if you observed anything different

about her—aside from her injuries."

"And aside from the cigarette burns?"

"Yes."

"Well, there was something. I didn't see it, but her mother told me about it later. I assume she already mentioned it to you."

"Maybe. Try me."

"Jen's silver locket."

"The one in her photo inscribed with a J?"

Ronnie nods. "It was missing."

"She was wearing it when she was abducted?"

"She always wore it," Ronnie replies. "Even when she surfed."

"Didn't she worry about losing it in the water?"

"You'd think so. But it was her good luck charm. She had the chain shortened so the locket couldn't come off her neck even when she wiped out.

"Hmmm. Her mother didn't mention that. I'm not sure the necklace was ever recovered. I'll check with her."

Ronnie gets a faraway look in his eyes. "If you find Jen's locket I'd sure like to have it."

"I assume her mother would too."

The corners of his mouth turn down. "Makes sense."

I snap a couple of shots of the cavern that once held the remains of Jennifer Reece, then we start back down the trail. I make a mental note about Jennifer's locket. It's another small thing that could lead nowhere. But you never know.

Ronnie next takes me to a similarly overgrown site nearby where Tara Marie Havens' body was found. He tells how all three hidden graves were discovered one after another on the same day. After Jennifer's body was located, Tara's remains were found. And then those of Elise Morneau. The proximity of the three makeshift graves became a powerful clue that Kauaʻi police were hunting a serial killer, the same assailant attacking three different women.

There's not much more to see at the two other gravesites. Ronnie remembers less about these two women than about the woman of his dreams.

He reminisces about Jennifer on the ride back to Waimea town. The ironman has misty eyes when he hops out at the Shrimp Shack. I thank him again and pull away watching him stand forlornly by the curb, as if he's still waiting for her. I feel qualms once more about enlisting his help. But I drive on—to Hanapepe and then to the West Side village of Eleʻele.

Just inland of Port Allen, where many of the Na Pali Coast boat tours depart, Eleʻele boasts the largest coffee farm in the islands and in the entire United States. There's also a small shopping center with a McDonald's, Subway, post office, and laundromat. But more important for the case—a women's clinic where Strangler victim Elise Morneau worked. I'm escorted into the office of the center's director Dawn Lee, RN, fortyish and well put together in green scrubs. She must frequent the gym.

"Elise and I were close friends," Director Lee begins. "We both started here as new RNs." She points to a photo on her desk—a group shot of a half-dozen young nurses in uniform. "I'm in the middle and that's Elise on the left," Director Lee points to the bobbed blonde with that same quirky smile in the photo Mrs. Reece showed me.

"She looks playful and happy."

"She was. So full of life and so grateful to have her first job at our clinic. Elise came from a large nurturing family in Michigan and was very idealistic. She wanted to help people. That's why she became a nurse. She was twenty-four and married when she started here. Her husband stayed on the mainland finishing his master's degree in hospital administration."

"She was the only married victim," I say, "from what I understand."

"Elise's husband, Jon, planned to join Elise and find employment on Kaua'i once he finished his degree. They were looking forward to starting a family. Until then letters, emails, and phone calls had to suffice. This was before social media and video chats. They saw each other in person infrequently because of the expense. They'd been married little more than two years and spent nearly half of that time apart."

"Then came the Strangler."

"Yes, unfortunately. I don't know whatever happened to Jon. He was shattered by Elise's death, as you can imagine. We kept in touch for a while. But I haven't heard from him in years."

"Sad for him. I hope he was finally able to put his life back together."

"We always think first, of course, about the victims of these vicious crimes," Dawn observes. "We don't always consider their family and friends and colleagues and neighbors who are also victimized, indirectly."

"Collateral damage. It's a phrase I find myself using repeatedly on this case."

"Anyway, Elise looked more like a high school senior than

a nursing school graduate. She was very active and bicycled everywhere—to work and shop, to visit friends, and to the beach."

"Wasn't she riding her bike on the night she disappeared?"

"Yes. She rode to meet a friend at a restaurant—a diner really, in Hanapepe."

"A male friend?"

"No, female. Her name was Marta and her life ended too soon, as well. But not at the hands of the Strangler. A few years ago she succumbed to pancreatic cancer."

"I'm sorry. I guess I can't interview Marta."

"You would have liked her. She was fine person like Elise."

"Back to Elise," I say, "what can you tell me about that night?"

"When Elise didn't show up, Marta used the diner's phone to call the clinic and was told by someone on the staff, I don't remember who, that Elise had left an hour before to pedal to dinner. Eventually Marta called the Kaua'i police."

"She must have been worried."

"Not only Marta, but also Elise's husband. That night Jon waited for a call from her. It never came. He phoned the clinic the next morning. Elise hadn't shown up for work, but nobody here knew what had happened to her."

"When did you find out?"

"Her abandoned bike was found later that morning but her remains, as you know, were not discovered until much later."

"I've just been to Waimea Canyon and saw what's left of her makeshift grave."

The director shakes her head. "I still can't believe it. Even after all these years."

"Do you recognize any of these men?" I show the director the five mugshots on my phone of the persons of interest.

"I've seen the photos before," she says, "but I never saw the Strangler suspects myself in person."

"How about this police sketch?" I show her the final image that is only a drawing.

She pauses. "He looks vaguely familiar. Like a man I saw in a Hanalei shop."

"Recently?"

"Yes, within the last few months."

"Do you remember which shop?"

"Sorry. No. And I doubt this could be the same man. It's been twenty years since that sketch."

"Do you remember anything else that you didn't recall when the police questioned you? Or has anything come to your attention that you didn't know about then? An overheard conversation? An offhand remark? An item of Elise's belatedly found or recovered? Anything that might shed light on the case?"

She pauses. "No, I don't think so. Well, wait a minute."

"Yes?"

"I don't know what made me think of this the other day after all these years, but before Elise mounted her bicycle that evening to pedal to Hanapepe for dinner she asked me if I had ever tried fajitas at the café. It served Mexican food, you know, back then. It's a completely different place now. Chinese. Fairly good."

"And what did you say?"

"I told Elise I hadn't, but I'd heard the fajitas were good. Elise said that decided it for her. She would order fajitas and tell me the next morning how they tasted. There wasn't a next morning for Elise. I never saw her again."

When the interview concludes with Director Lee, I climb back into my rented Jeep and head for the Hanapepe diner Elise Morneau never made it to that fateful evening. I'm going to investigate the Chinese restaurant where the Mexican diner used to be. Not for the case. For my dinner. It's getting late and I haven't eaten since breakfast on Oʻahu.

On the short drive I reflect on what I have learned about Elise Morneau. Her colleague and friend, Eleʻele Center Director Dawn Lee, colored in details of Elise's life I could have gleaned only from a firsthand source, making Elise's premature and violent death seem all the more poignant and the Strangler himself all the more despicable. I'm not sure at this point how much it helps the case—except to provide another example of how the killer targeted a loving and resourceful young woman who had much to give the world. Of course, her human qualities would have meant nothing to him.

I had known already that Elise was the Strangler's only married victim, but not that her husband was on the mainland. I also knew she had ridden her bicycle to an eatery in Hanapepe. I didn't know it was Mexican or that she planned to order fajitas. More miscellaneous facts. The rest of the story I did know. Elise's bicycle was recovered the next morning, but not Elise herself until several weeks later, in a makeshift grave in Waimea Canyon where I'd just visited. Dawn Lee did not recognize any of photos I showed her of persons of interest. But she did think she'd seen a man who resembled the police sketch in a Hanalei shop. Something, at least, I can follow up on.

That evening in a Hanapepe B&B after a phone call to Vivienne—she's feeling better, thankfully—I watch local election results on TV. Janson Newfield is edging out incumbent prosecutor Buddy Kalaheo—as the polls predicted—by a razor thin margin. I wonder again if the disappearance of Newfield's daughter has given him a sympathy boost against a popular incumbent. The tally is so close the sitting prosecutor hasn't yet conceded.

eight

Wednesday morning I drive back to the Garden Isle's largest town, Līhu'e. On the radio the big story is Janson Newfield's narrow victory over Kalaheo. The incumbent is calling for a recount.

Līhu'e has a population of around seven thousand and is the home of island commerce, government, and major air and shipping ports. But for most visitors Līhu'e is not so much a destination as a springboard to other island destinations. I'm an exception. I'm heading there to the island's institution of higher education.

Off Kaumuali'i Highway on the outskirts of Līhu'e, Kaua'i Community College spreads over green acres of tidy red-roofed buildings resembling a gentrified hobby farm. I leg it across some of that green to the offices of college administration. I'm expected by Vice Chancellor of Student Affairs, Dr. Gwen Kalama, who knew Strangler victim Tara Marie Havens.

Wearing an orchid dress and infectious smile, Dr. Kalama gives off a positive vibe. I'm encouraged to expect she'll be helpful. But when I ask about Tara Havens, the Vice

Chancellor's smile fades.

"Tara was a free spirit who may have unknowingly put herself at risk," says Dr. Kalama in pleasant tones. "I was her sociology teacher during her freshman year. The reason I remember her so well was her singing. Her first semester she joined a local band that landed a steady gig at a Hanalei bar. Tara sang with a Janis Joplin bluesy verve that made you sit up and listen. Before long she had a following."

"Was her singing in a band what you meant by her being a free spirit?"

"More than that. Tara had a mind of her own. She did what she wanted. And she was pretty."

"I've seen her photo," I reply. "Raven hair and dark eyes."

"She weighed barely one hundred pounds. Still a child, in many ways."

"Do you think Tara's working in a bar put her at risk?"

Dr. Kalama nods. "Not only that. Tara sometimes hitchhiked to her gig."

"Prison inmates will tell you," I reply, "never climb into the car of someone you don't know. Once you're inside the bad guys have you."

"Tara was Tara. Nobody was going to tell her what to do."

"Do you know if she was dating?"

"I heard she dated a few guys. One was a bandmate. She partied with the band. And she often missed classes after her gigs. Once she missed an entire week."

"Is that why when she disappeared nobody noticed at first?"

"To me it seemed like just another extended absence."

"Can you tell me about the bandmate she dated? And anyone else?"

"They were all investigated by Kaua'i police. Well, except one."

"Which one was that?"

"A guy apparently named Josh. He wasn't a KCC student. Police couldn't track him down, from what I understand. I've always wondered about him."

"Did Josh look like any of these?" On my phone I show Dr. Kalama the photos and police sketch.

"I never saw Josh," she says, "only heard about him from one of her bandmates after the fact."

"Do you recognize any of them?"

She looks at all six images. She squints. The corners of her mouth turn down. "I wish I did, but I don't."

"Anything else you can remember?"

"Tara told friends she thought someone had been following her. She had seen an orange VW Beetle behind her two or three times but didn't know if by coincidence. That was strange because Tara had no qualms about jumping into almost any vehicle, as I told you. But this Beetle gave her pause."

"And she saw the Beetle several times?"

"That's what I heard."

"If that was the Strangler's car and Tara climbed in . . ." I stop myself.

"We'll probably never know," replies Dr. Kalama. "And I'm sure Kaua'i Police investigated."

"No doubt. Anything else you can tell me about Tara?"

"When she disappeared her mother contacted the college and her inquiry was directed to me. Mrs. Havens was a working single mom and she was worried. She said her daughter was a good girl, but a merrymaker who liked to kick up her heels. Talented and smart, but a classic underachiever."

"I know the type. Bright and creative young people can become bored by school."

"Her mother also said Tara had been sheltered most of her life and was too trusting. She considered the world a safe place and didn't understand that a beautiful young woman needs to be vigilant."

"Her mother was right," I reply. "Did you ever hear from Mrs. Havens again?"

"Yes, after Tara's body was found Mrs. Havens reminisced that her daughter had been full of life. And she shared that fullness with others. Her mother couldn't comprehend the evil of a man who would take advantage of such a sweet and joyful person."

"I can't either," I reply. "And I'm in the business."

I thank Dr. Kalama and then head north up the winding two-lane coastal highway named for Hawaiian royalty, Prince Jonah Kūhiō Kalaniana'ole, toward the former plantation town of Kilauea. Passing the seaside hamlets of Wailua, Kapa'a and Anahola, I consider what I learned at Kaua'i Community College. Tara Marie Havens—free spirit, band singer, and hitchhiker—may have put herself in harm's way. At the time of her abduction she had been dating one of the men never accounted for. Could he have been the one? Not if the Strangler followed the usual pattern of serial killers. He would not have known her, nor she him. Unless of course the Strangler was atypical. Did he go by the name Josh and drive an orange VW Beetle?

In Kilauea, whose historic lighthouse marks the northernmost point of all inhabited Hawaiian Islands, I pull up to a sprawling home tastefully sited on five gently sloping acres overlooking the sea. It's the home of Alana Newfield's family, the young woman who has been missing since Halloween. Thanks to my attorney friend Tommy Woo, I have an in with her father, Janson Newfield III, Kauaʻi County Prosecutor-elect, though sitting prosecutor Buddy Kalaheo still hasn't conceded and is calling for a recount. Newfield campaigned on solving several decades-old cold cases—the most prominent being the Barking Sands Strangler.

I'm interested in talking with him for that reason. What does he know about the Strangler that I don't? He might not have bothered to see me. But his daughter has gone missing, I'm a private detective investigating the Strangler murders, and my investigation could potentially uncover something pertaining to his daughter's disappearance. In other words, we might be able to help each other.

The attorney comes off in person, as in his campaign ads, as ambitious, tough, and determined. But he's showing signs of strain. His face is drawn. It's been several days since Alana vanished. When I arrive he's still trying to comfort his obviously shaken wife. While his face betrays stress, hers looks as pale and immobile as a mask. Mrs. Newfield manages to say hello through a numbness no doubt shielding unbearable pain. Her husband's attempts to comfort her show little results.

Newfield leads me into a wood-paneled den where we sit and talk. Or, more precisely, *he* talks. He tells me about his daughter in intimate detail because, I assume, he wants me to help find her.

"The reason Alana abruptly returned home from college during October of her senior year," her father explains, "was a traumatic breakup with her boyfriend. Then on Halloween night she went out and never returned. I reported her missing. But I think I know why she disappeared. The criminal element afraid of my election to prosecuting attorney. Or worse, the Barking Sands Strangler himself is active again and targeting my own family."

"Would that be likely, sir, after twenty years?"

"Ten years, if you count the unsolved murder of Amity Johnson."

"You're suggesting the Strangler may still be on the island and has come out of hibernation?"

"Yes, I'm suggesting."

"Since no kidnap note has been found, sir, could Alana have simply run away? Maybe back to her boyfriend in Seattle?"

Newfield slowly shakes his head.

"Or could she have—I hesitate to even mention it—in desperation taken her own life?"

"None of that is likely," Newfield replies. "I'm afraid my daughter has been abducted."

"Do you have evidence?"

"I can't comment," the attorney replies. "But for now, we'll continue to search for Alana on the Garden Isle. Not likely she's gone back to her boyfriend. He's been questioned and is being watched."

I don't bother to show Newfield photos of the six suspects because he's no doubt seen their mugs. And I don't mention Alana's arrest in Seattle. But I do wonder if Newfield knows.

"Sorry to rush off." Newfield rises. "Press conference.

About my election, you know? That SOB Kalaheo still hasn't conceded."

He gives me his card, which already lists him as county prosecutor, and then says, "Let me know immediately if you find anything. This is not only personal—but professional. I'm the county prosecutor. My daughter's missing."

I don't much like Newfield's tone but answer, "Fair enough."

When Newfield departs I talk briefly with his wife Margaret Anne, who even through her pain resembles the newspaper photo of her attractive daughter in all but age. Mrs. Newfield appears in no shape to talk. Her two younger daughters, Noe and Pualei, whose features favor their father, only softer, surround her. The two girls may know more about what happened to their sister, or at least why, than either their mother or their father. But I don't press them. Or their mother. I try to respect their privacy in this time of distress. In the very unlikely event Alana's disappearance descends into the horror her father fears I may need to come again.

From the Newfields' Kilauea retreat I drive further on Kūhiō Highway, past the golf links and sea-cliff resorts of Princeville to the north shore town of Hanalei. Hanalei is one of my favorite spots in all the islands. Majestic mountain backdrop. Lovely crescent bay. Picturesque covered pier. Awesome surf breaks. Local-style and trendy shops and eateries. Hanalei has it all. Not to mention lively nightlife where locals and visitors alike can enjoy a craft brew and a local band—like the one Tara Marie Havens fronted.

What chance do I have to spot the man clinic director Dawn Lee thought resembled the police sketch? A lead is a lead. I can't afford to pass on any. I hop out and walk around the village showing the composite police sketch of the unnamed suspect in the Barking Sands murders.

I step into a few pint-sized shops whose staffs appear to be mostly off-duty surfers. I ask if they've seen the man in the police sketch, explaining that twenty years have passed since the sketch was drawn. I get what you'd expect. Over and over. One waitress in a diner finds the face vaguely familiar but can't remember from where or when.

About to call it quits, I step into a kayak rental shop and show the sketch to a young clerk who would have been a baby when the murders took place. He's in shorts revealing his surfer's knobby knees.

"That's my boss," he says.

"Really?"

"Only kidding," the surfer says. "I like to pull his chain."

"What's his name?"

"Mr. Boz."

"Boz? Like '70s pop singer Boz Skaggs?"

"No, like Ian Boz."

"May I speak with him?"

"He's not here. And he's not the guy. He's married and has two grown kids and a cute little terrier."

"Well, that doesn't mean . . ." I start to say, but he cuts me off.

"And a lot of people think he looks like someone else."

I hand the surfer my card, ask him to have his boss call me, and go on my way.

Driving back to Līhuʻe Airport I wonder again about Tara singing in a Hanalei bar. Could this be where the Strangler targeted her?

nine

Thursday morning after a welcome home with Vivienne I'm back on Maunakea Street. I arrive early before the *lei* shop opens and find a homeless man sleeping in Mrs. Fujiyama's doorway. He's sunburned and grizzled and has some nasty sores on his exposed limbs. A few pieces of cardboard serve as his pillow and yesterday's newspaper as a makeshift blanket. His soiled and ripped garb smells of urine. Just then he wakes, rolls to one side, and pees in the doorway. I watch the yellow stream descend onto the sidewalk and then trickle over the curbing and into the gutter.

This is Chinatown these days. Public urination. Sex on the sidewalks. Drugs. Not to mention theft and assault. Homelessness has grown exponentially here since a sit-lie ban went into effect in Waikīkī. Every time the homeless are cleared from one area they move to another. It's a problem we grapple with every day. Hawai'i's temperate climate beckons people who'd rather spend a winter's night on balmy Maunakea Street than on a frigid boulevard in New York City. As the gap between rich and poor widens, homelessness is up not only in Hawai'i but elsewhere in America.

The homeless man goes back to sleep. I pull a twenty from my wallet and slip it under his cardboard pillow. I know what they say about giving money to panhandlers. But that's not this man. He's not begging. And he hasn't got a pot to pee in. Or a roof over his head or decent clothes to cover his backside. If I'm wrong, so be it. He may go buy a bottle of gin with my twenty. It's his money now. He can do with it what he likes. Rather than step over him I hike around to the back of the shop and climb the outdoor stairs to the second-floor offices. If Mrs. Fujiyama needs my help moving him when she arrives later, she knows she can count on me. Or she can contact the private security firm that Chinatown merchants employ. Or call the HPD substation on the next block of Maunakea Street.

At the top of the stairs a familiar musty smell floats into the hallway when I unlock the two dead bolts and swing open the thick mahogany door that says SURFING DETECTIVE: CONFIDENTIAL INVESTIGATIONS—ALL ISLANDS, beneath that hanging-ten board rider. I put in this solid wood door and the dead bolts myself because the late Mr. Fujiyama, when he built these offices, used hollow-core doors with cheap knob-locks. The locks were a joke. A common kitchen knife could spring them. As for the hollow-core doors, any able-bodied woman or man could easily punch their fist through.

My office is about the size and sturdiness of a Cracker Jack box, containing my battleship grey desk, a Naugahyde client's chair, and a rusting file cabinet with my longboard trophy sitting on top, and my one window overlooking the bustle and fading charm of storied old Maunakea Street. I open the window and let in the sweet fragrance of ginger blossom wafting up from the *lei* shop below amid the sharper competing odors of Chinatown: kim chee, espresso, the fishy scent of the morning's catch, cigarette smoke, incense, rancid garbage, hot malasadas, roast duck and, more often these days, urine.

My phone message light is blinking. Tommy Woo. He skips his usual obligatory joke.

"Hey Kai, Ossendorfer, Noboru, and Chang expects the go-ahead from Detroit early next week on that Maui accident suit . . ."

Good news. If my Garden Isle case runs out of leads, Matt Ossendorfer waits in the wings.

About an hour later, right on time, there's a knock on my door.

"Morning, Mrs. Reece." I'm expecting her. She tries for a smile that barely reaches the corners of her mouth. But the lines on her face look softer, as if she's opened a new, more promising chapter in her story of pain.

"Good morning, Kai." She says then gets right to the point. "What did you find on Kaua'i?"

"Little things." I look into her expectant eyes. "I stopped first at KPD headquarters and spoke with the officer in charge of cold cases, Detective Ellen Nakamura."

"I remember her," Marian Reece says.

"And she remembers you."

Mrs. Reece nods and tries that smile again.

"Ellen couldn't tell me anything, as I expected, but she referred me to a retired officer who could. Ernie Hong was on the force when the Strangler murders happened. Ernie shared photos with me of six suspects. Well, one of the six was only a police sketch. And Ernie recalled another person who was never pursued because he had no record and worked in island government. This man lived on the West Side where the murders began and could still live there. But Ernie couldn't remember his name or address. Or even what town the man lived in."

"Detective Hong thought the Strangler could be someone not among the six?"

"Possibly. Which would mean that whoever committed these crimes and has gotten away with them all these years may be cleverer than any of those six."

"Sounds like Detective Hong has given us a step forward."

"We'll see."

"Did you meet with Ronnie?"

"Yes. I drove Ronnie to Polihale State Park and to Waimea Canyon and asked him about the man who abducted Jennifer. Ronnie saw him but couldn't make out his facial features. Before this happened Jennifer had dated a guy named Mitch. Ronnie wasn't happy about Mitch. He said Kaua'i police searched for him after Jen went missing but he never turned up."

"Do you think Ronnie is still in love with Jenny?"

"No question," I reply. "He was broken up revisiting the last place he ever saw her."

Mrs. Reece sighs. "Those two would have made beautiful babies. My grandchildren. I wonder what they would have looked like. Would they have taken after Jennifer and my family? Or after Ronnie and his? I'll never know."

I listen. I try to understand. Then I say: "I'm sorry. It's not the same thing exactly but when I was just a small kid I lost both parents in a small plane crash."

"Terrible!" She says this like she really means it. "That must have had a profound effect on you."

"One day my mom and dad were alive, the next they weren't. I can't change what happened to them or to your daughter. But maybe I can turn up something that will at least make progress on this very cold case."

"I'm confident you will."

"Speaking of turning up things, when Ronnie and I hiked into Waimea Canyon he remembered the heart-shaped silver locket Jennifer was wearing in her graduation photo."

"What about it? I gave her that locket and had it engraved. I haven't seen it since she died."

"Ronnie said Jenny wore the silver heart all the time, even when she surfed. But when her body was discovered it was gone."

"It couldn't have fallen off?"

"Not according to Ronnie," I reply. "He said she shortened the chain so that the locket wouldn't come off."

"Then she deliberately took it off? Or someone else did?"

"Could be." I don't mention that serial killers sometimes take souvenirs or mementos from their victims.

Mrs. Reece's glances down. "I don't want to think about that."

I change the subject. "I also interviewed people who knew the other two victims: Elise Morneau and Tara Marie Havens."

My client looks up again.

"I visited a clinic in Ele'ele and spoke with center director Dawn Lee, who knew Elise, and stopped by Kaua'i

Community College and interviewed Dr. Gwen Kalama, who remembered Tara. Director Lee thought she saw the man in the police sketch in Hanalei, which is the same place Dr. Kalama told me Tara sang in a band. It could be just a coincidence, but I went to Hanalei and showed the sketch around. A clerk in a kayak rental shop pinned him as his own boss. But the boss wasn't there. I'll look him up when I return to Kaua'i."

"That does sound curious."

"Oh, and Tara had dated a guy named Josh. But her Josh, like Jennifer's Mitch, has never been found."

"How about the girl who recently went missing?" Mrs. Reece asks.

"I spoke to her family. They live in Kilauea and the girl's father, as you know, is the County Prosecutor-elect on the Garden Isle. Janson Newfield suspects his daughter was abducted as a vendetta against him. He's convinced she didn't just go missing or return to her boyfriend in Seattle."

Mrs. Reece looks concerned. "Do you think there's any connection between his daughter's disappearance and Jennifer's?"

"Nothing links the two cases at this point. Except maybe in Newfield's mind."

"I hope you're right—for his family's sake."

I shrug. "There's always the chance that the Strangler crimes could have been committed by a transient type we've not much considered: a tourist sex offender, an active military or vet with PTSD, a violent homeless person, or various kinds of criminals who roam the islands. But I'm inclined to agree with Ernie. We may be led to someone who's been on the island all this time, but off the radar."

Mrs. Reece rises and hugs me. "Thank you, Kai! It's a start."

She glances up at the trophy on my filing cabinet and in a lighter mood asks, "Did you win that?" Before I can answer she reads the inscription aloud: "Third Place—Classic Longboard—Mākaha."

"Years ago, I competed in a local contest at Mākaha. The waves were cranking that day. Boards were snapping like toothpicks. In the final round I got lucky and one teeth-rattling ride positioned me, I thought, to win it all. But on that same wave—the wave *of my life*—my nearest competitor got hit by his board going over the falls. I kicked out and paddled to him. And it's a good thing I did. He was out—knocked unconscious. Long story short, neither of us took home first prize. He got second and I got this." I point to the tarnished trophy.

"That trophy says a lot about you," Mrs. Reece replies.

"That I have rotten luck?"

"No. That you're a good human being."

"Thanks, but I paddled for him instinctively. That was my first and only contest. I wasn't good enough and, anyway, competition is not why I surf."

She slowly nods.

"Back to the case. We have a few leads taking us in different directions. They may ultimately go nowhere. That's the chance we take."

"I'm willing to take that chance. I have nothing else left to live for."

After Marian Reece departs I decide to dig deeper into the disappearance of Janson Newfield's daughter. It may have nothing to do with Jennifer's death twenty years ago, but in the unlikely event Newfield's suspicions about Alana's vanishing are not as farfetched as they appear, the two young women's plights could be connected.

I want to answer two questions about Alana Newfield: First, why was she arrested in Seattle? And second, why did she abruptly return home during her senior year in college? I try my trusted online sources and get some results, but not the gritty details I need. Those require boots on the ground in Seattle. Since it's not feasible to put my own boots down in the Emerald City, given that Alana's disappearance is only a side issue at this point, I phone Seattle PI Kitty Stockwell.

"Kai! How are things in Paradise?" Kitty's booming voice, as usual, inspires confidence. She's my go-to agent in the Pacific Northwest. She's good at what she does.

"Can't complain."

"You better not," she replies. "It's been raining here for a week."

"Condolences," I say. "Reason I'm calling is I wondered if you could give me a hand."

"Would this include a trip to Hawai'i?" Kitty laughs. "You know, get me out of this Seattle soup for a while?"

"Actually, the help I need is in Seattle. But maybe a trip to the islands next time?"

"I'll hold you to it, Kai. Now what can I do for you?"

I tell Kitty about Alana Newfield's arrest and her abruptly dropping out of St. Ursula College in her senior year. Alana had attended the church-affiliated school her entire college career and then suddenly she bolts. Why?

"Her parents claim a breakup with her longtime boyfriend as the reason, Kitty. I'm not convinced they're telling the truth."

"Or maybe their daughter wasn't telling them the truth?"

"Could be. Would you look into it for me? Maybe go to the college and try to sort it out?"

"I can do that. How deep do you want to go?"

"This is a sideline to my own investigation," I explain, "so for now just why Alana was arrested and why she left school. Please send me your usual hourly bill."

"You're on, Kai!" Kitty replies. "Next time you're flying me to Paradise."

"Anything I can do for a fellow PI."

"I'll hold you to it."

ten

After the call with Kitty I walk past the offices of my four fellow tenants—a free-lance editor, a bookkeeper, a passport photographer, and Madame Zenobia, the psychic, a.k.a. Shirley Schwartz. I hurry by the beaded curtain in Shirley's doorway and the pungent incense wafting into the hallway. Last thing I need today is the bejeweled Madame telling my fortune.

I step down the orange shag stairs into the ambrosial fragrances of colorful island flowers: pale yellow plumeria, cream-colored *pīkake*, fire red *lehua,* orange *'ilima,* purple orchid, bone-white tuberose, lavender crown flower, green *maile*, yellow ginger. *Lucky you live Hawai'i.* Mrs. Fujiyama stands at her register—bone-thin, steel-haired, barely five feet tall—ringing up a customer with two tuberose *lei.* She glances up at me over her half-glasses with her usual courteous smile and says, "Good morning, Mr. Cooke."

"Morning, Mrs. Fujiyama." I smile back.

We are on the most cordial terms, Mrs. Fujiyama and I. Though she maintains a businesslike distance between herself and her tenants, I've gotten closer than most because I help her out now and then. When the parolee ex-boyfriend of her *lei* girl Blossom kept dropping by the shop and harassing her I helped send him back to prison, though it cost me an ambulance ride to Queens Hospital. I glance over at the worktable and see Blossom—free now from Junior—and Chastity and Joon stringing ginger in their pink t-shirts that say FUJIYAMA'S FLOWER LEIS. Keeping my office above a *lei* shop has its advantages aside from the beautiful blossoms and fragrances: it offers my clients a degree of anonymity. They can linger among the *lei* and then slip unnoticed upstairs. Even if they are seen, they've got four other excuses for being there. A fortune told by Madame Zenobia? A passport photo? And so on. Anonymity is no small thing, since most people coming to see me don't want that fact known.

When I step out the doorway the homeless man and his cardboard pillow and newspaper blanket are gone. A faint urine smell remains. I gaze up at Mrs. Fujiyama's building. My window overlooking Maunakea Street is open. My office is the only one with a window, not to mention the roomiest. Maybe Mrs. Fujiyama really does favor me? She owns this decaying pre-war specimen with dazzling ornaments of an Asian cast—two-headed dragons, serpents, wild boars, and ancient Chinese characters spelling a mysterious message in red. I asked a friend who knew some Chinese what the words meant. She scratched her head and said that some puzzles are best left unsolved. Frankly, I think she just couldn't decipher it. But I haven't bothered to ask anyone else who knows the language.

I hike to my car in a Maunakea Street garage, stepping around another homeless person sprawled in another shop doorway, her bare legs and soiled skirt extending onto the sidewalk. I count my blessings. I have job, a roof over my head, a car, and a covered stall to park it in. Parking is no small thing in Chinatown. Mrs. Fujiyama reserves three stalls for her tenants. Five tenants and only three stalls. Again, I'm one of the lucky ones.

At the garage I slide into my vintage Impala. I bought the teal blue '69 Chevy from a widow whose late husband purchased it new at Aloha Motors, a defunct dealership formerly on the site of the Hawai'i Convention Center. With less than 50,000 original miles, four-on-the-floor, and a 427 cubic-inch Turbo Jet V8, this baby really rocks. And with the back seat popped out, my longboard slides right in. That's the beauty of these outsized classic cars—a genuine gas-guzzling dream machine from the sixties. *The real thing.* I feel guilty pumping so much petrol into this puppy—not to mention my wallet crying *ouch.* Plus, PIs normally drive nondescript vehicles that escape notice. I keep thinking about parting with her but haven't had the heart yet to let her go.

Soon my Impala is growling along Ala Moana Boulevard, the nose of my surfboard resting comfortably on the padded teal dash. I drive a few blocks to the Kaka'ako campus of Paradise College. Thanks to a referral from Vivienne I have an appointment with a professor of psychology who specializes in criminal minds. I want to learn more about what makes a serial killer tick. Better yet, I want to learn more about what makes the Barking Sands Strangler tick. If anybody can tell me, it's Professor Bernard Strohmeyer.

I arrive early for my appointment and stroll the grassy quad, aiming toward the office of Professor Strohmeyer. The small liberal arts college sits on the water's edge, lending itself more to the rush of surfing than to the rigors of higher education. Maybe that's just me? Wave rider. College dropout.

I step up to the art deco building housing the Department of Psychology and climb outside stairs to the second floor. With a few minutes to spare I stop at a landing and take in the view of my favorite surf spot in Kakaʻako Waterfront Park called Flies. A nice set is rolling in. That decides it. After work, surfing today at Flat Island with my buddy Kula.

I finally tear myself away. Just a few doors down from the headquarters of the psychology department I pop into the office of an aloha-shirted gentleman in his sixties, desk piled high with books and papers. The professor's eyes are frosty blue like Santa Claus's. His full white beard cements the impression. I hope he's got gifts for me in the form of information that will help me with the case.

"Professor Strohmeyer?" I hand him my card. "Kai Cooke. Professor Vivienne Duvane referred me."

"If Vivienne sent you, you must be all right." He glances at the card. "Surfing Detective? Didn't you help Serena Wright with that regrettable problem in Paris?" He's referring to the Director of the International Studies Program.

"I did."

"I like to think we have fewer criminals per capita in our student population than in the general population, but that homicide in Paris makes me wonder." The professor shakes his head. "Imagine hanging a fellow student in his dorm room!"

"That was sad. And I'm afraid I've come to you for help with another sad case involving the death of promising young person . . ." I pause. "The Barking Sands Strangler. Do you remember him, Professor Strohmeyer?"

"I do," he replies. "And please call me Bernie."

"Mahalo, Bernie. If you remember the Strangler, you know that twenty years ago three young women disappeared on the island of Kaua'i and were later found murdered with a wave image cigarette-burned into their breasts. These horrible crimes have never been solved. They've been cold cases for two decades."

"Barking Sands is the name the Strangler actually gave himself," Bernie declares, "in a communication with a local television station."

"I didn't see that in anything I read so far."

"Serial killers often have tremendous egos, you know, and self-aggrandizement is part of their game. I suspect, too, that he might have been trying to lead investigators astray. Did he want them to think he lived and operated in that locale, an area mostly of beaches and agricultural land and little population? Anyway, we haven't seen many serial killers in Hawai'i— well, except for the Honolulu Strangler even longer ago—so I've been following the Barking Sands case for years."

"The mother of one of the three victims hired me to investigate. She believes she'll never find lasting peace until the Strangler is brought to account. She doesn't use the word justice because she doesn't believe justice can ever be done."

"I understand," he says.

"So, here's my problem, Bernie. This is my first serial killer case. I've already started investigating on Kaua'i, but I know little about the breed except the notorious ones."

"Like Ted Bundy, Wayne Gacy, Jeffrey Dahmer, The Son of Sam, and the BTK and the Golden State killers?" he replies.

"If you know about these you may already know more than most people."

"Knowing even more could help. That's where you come in."

Strohmeyer scratches his white beard. "Okay, let's start with what a serial killer is not."

I sit back and hope the lesson I need is coming.

"A serial killer is not a one-off murderer, the type who kills an individual person on impulse or for money or power or protection or revenge. The victim of a one-off killer is often someone the murderer knows and is even close to, like a spouse or girlfriend or coworker or boss. The victims of serial killers, on the other hand, are typically unknown to the killer."

"That must make serial killers hard to track?"

"Precisely." The professor shifts in his chair. "A serial killer is also not a mass murderer. Mass murderers kill several people, usually all in one place and at the same time. Mass murders are sometimes labeled terrorist attacks, if the killer or killers have political motivations. In the United States we have gotten all too used to mass shootings, especially in schools and churches and workplaces. But more often than not, the killer in these cases has no real political agenda, rather a personal vendetta, mental illness, or some dark, sadistic, suicidal desire for renown."

"A waste of innocent lives."

"Sadly," the professor says. "For serial killers, in contrast to one-off murderers and mass murderers, killing is in their DNA. They have a built-in ongoing need to kill and will go on killing until they are stopped. Sometimes there may be a lull in the murders. The perpetrator may take a week, a month, or even years off."

"Sounds like the Strangler."

"The murders on Kauaʻi were the killing of individual victims of similar type and in similar situations over a period of one summer. The Strangler could have remained on Kauaʻi undetected."

"How about the one-time prime suspect now at Halawa, Theron Walter?"

"If it's Walter the killing stopped because he went to prison. If it's not, the killer may have simply gone dormant, as some serial killers do for various reasons—growing older, life and work changes, and so on. But he could possibly become active again."

"Do you remember the murder of Amity Johnson ten years after the first three victims? Could that have been the work of the Strangler?"

"Possible, but not likely if Kauaʻi police didn't find any close similarities."

"Her remains were apparently too far gone to show his signature."

The professor nods. "So we can't rule out the Strangler."

"What happened to this guy that made him so deranged?"

"There's some debate. A brain injury or mental illness could be the cause. But more often it's nurture rather than nature. In my opinion."

"How so?"

"Most serial killers have troubled childhoods. They may be victims, at a tender age, of neglect and physical and sexual abuse. Or they may witness abuse between members of their household. One particular adult may scar them. The child may carry a vendetta against the offender into adulthood. Because of the abuse and violence they experience, these unfortunate children fail to develop love, trust, and empathy. Nor do they learn how to interact in positive ways with others."

"Not good for their later lives."

"Exactly. They show disturbing tendencies before long. As teenagers they may set fires, threaten others with knives, exhibit cruelty to animals. They develop little or no regard for the rights of others and no sense, really, of anybody but themselves. They lack conscience. Their behavior may seem purposeless and irrational to the rest of us. It's a condition called ASPD, antisocial personality disorder—similar to the term sociopathy. Sociopathy and psychopathy are basically interchangeable, but most researchers prefer the term psychopathy."

"I've run into people like this in my line of work."

"They start young," the professor replies. "It's not uncommon for serial killers to have arrest records dating back to their juvenile years. They grow into adulthood and may appear to function normally, but their apparent feelings and concerns for others are only an act, modeled on behavior they observe. Your serial killer is a great manipulator—a user of people. Only *his* needs and feelings matter. He carries a terrible childhood secret that left him with simmering anger. Sooner or later something triggers him to start taking revenge, typically on someone who represents, or stands in for, the one he most fears and reviles."

"Our Strangler fits the pattern?"

"Right. What we had on Kaua'i appears to be a sexual

sadist and psychopath, a lust killer. For him, the suffering of a woman is not just enjoyable but intensely arousing. It's a perversion of the erotic instinct, where one associates sexual pleasure with murder. In some strange way this is how the killer achieves intimacy. The sadism may have started as a fantasy, imagined harm done to a victim, the desire for sexual or psychological domination of another person. Then it moved to acts that range from humiliating behavior to criminal and potentially deadly crimes."

"Sounds like a sad, twisted individual."

"Afraid so. Because these women were all of a similar age and appearance and race, the killer—probably in his twenties or thirties when the crimes were committed—may have had something in for women of this type, even if he didn't know these women personally. If you could go back into his life, as I suggested, you may find that a woman of the victims' general description played some pivotal role. But not in a good way. The hurt he felt first happened at a young age. But he may have been hurt again as an adult—a woman of his dreams who broke up with him or cheated on him."

"The Strangler can meanwhile live an outwardly normal life?"

"Since he's gone without being caught all these years, yes, I would think he passes as a normal person who might be married with children, hold down a regular job, etc. He may be a known and respected figure. He may even work in law enforcement or a related field. That's, of course, if he's still on Kaua'i. Twenty years is a long time. Did he leave the island? Is he dead? Or if he is still on the Garden Isle, why did he take time off from killing for all these years?"

"How would he live two distinctly separate lives?"

"We used to call it MPD or multiple personality disorder, when individuals have at least one alter-personality which functions more or less independently. The more recent term is dissociative identity disorder. Simply put, the person deals with conflicting feelings and thoughts, often severe trauma from their early childhood, by repressing and compartmentalizing them into a separate personality. Having multiple personalities makes it unnecessary to reconcile these conflicting thoughts and feelings. Ted Bundy is a good example."

"I heard Bundy was charming."

"He was! A sensitive, caring volunteer at a suicide help line, a promising law student, a campaign coordinator for the reelection of a Republican governor, and a charismatic, dashing fellow who had no problem attracting women. But he had another personality."

"Ted Bundy—the charming serpent?"

"He obviously had to appear charming to lure the young women he abducted. None of them would have gone with him otherwise. He gained their confidence. They suspended their normal caution. He was above suspicion. Even people closest to him did not suspect him of the serial murders he committed."

"People are like waves," I say.

"What's that?" Professor Strohmeyer raises his brows.

"It's a saying from surfing that fits Bundy. Waves on the surface may sparkle and gleam, but look out below. Under that luminous green barrel hides a jagged reef—one heartbeat beneath the rushing foam—that can rip a board rider to pieces."

"Oh, kind of like Satan wearing a comely face?"

"Hmmm. So how do we catch this Satan with a comely face? Or, more to the point, how do we catch the Barking Sands Strangler?"

The Professor shrugs. "I wish I could help you there, Kai. The serial killer, as I mentioned, is one of the hardest criminals to catch. His victims are typically anonymous. There's no previous connection between predator and prey. He may stalk them but doesn't know them."

We talk more on the subject and then I bring up the recent disappearance of Alana Newfield. Her mention prompts the professor to reiterate an important point.

"Alana Newfield may fit the pattern in every way—but she disappeared twenty years later. It's a similar question to that of Amity Johnson. Has the Strangler come out of retirement twice in two decades?"

"And, for now, Alana is only missing, not murdered."

"Let's hope it stays that way," the professor replies.

"Let's hope she's found soon—and alive."

eleven

After the interview with Bernie Strohmeyer I head home pondering what the white-bearded professor of psychology had to say about serial killers. He's given me some new information to digest. I have a better sense of what motivated the Barking Sands Strangler. Even if I still find it hard to fathom the depth of his depravity.

Back on the Windward side, as I promised myself, I take Kula surfing at Flat Island. Before we hop on I rub my board down with my favorite wax. Don't ask me why they call it Sex Wax. Expressly for warm water, this milky pastel blue coconut-scented wax is about the size and shape of a hockey puck and its ambrosial fragrance never fails to rev me up. Kula loves it too. For him, the sniff of Sex Wax means, *Go surf, brah!*

After applying a generous coating of wax and saying my mantra I stroke us toward the tiny coral island a quarter mile offshore of Kailua Beach Park. As the golden boy hunches on the nose in front of me, the isle's four oblong acres resembling a table top come into view. Barely above the high tide mark, Flat Island—called Popoi'a or "fish rot" by Hawaiians—is today a bird sanctuary where mating seabirds nest in *pukas* or cubbyholes in the coral. The lee side of the island lies calm as glass. The water is crystal clear. I gaze down upon the sea bottom, the coral-studded floor sparkling like stars in the sky, and am reminded of Vivienne. Despite my serial killer investigation, she's never far from my thoughts.

I met Vivienne Duvane one night years ago at a Paradise College party and the next morning gave her a surf lesson in Waikīkī. The scarlet-haired professor of French arrived with her trim, athletic body adorned in an Olympic-style suit that took my breath away. She announced, "I'll show you what a woman can do," and promptly stood up on her very first wave. *Totally stoked.* She tumbled on her second wave, went under, and I dove down after her. We surfaced together clutching each other, our lips locked. A wave rolled over us. We didn't care. We kept at it, wondering what had just happened.

After that surf lesson we were together every night for a week until she broke the news that she was leaving for a yearlong fellowship in Brussels. We said our tearful goodbyes and promised to stay in touch. I did. She didn't.

My pride was hurt. I had no idea I was so forgettable.

Eventually I got over her. Then, years later, I took that unlikely case in Paris that Dr. Strohmeyer mentioned, and Professor Vivienne *Stone*—no longer Duvane—was provided by Paradise College, who had referred the case, as my translator and escort. Vivienne was solo in Paris, her husband having stayed behind. We reunited in a sidewalk café just steps from the Pantheon, under glowing heat lamps against an early April chill. She was as lovely as I remembered, in chic Parisian black rather than aloha attire. I breathed in the rosebud scent of her elegant perfume and fixed on the big rock on her ring finger. She ordered two glasses of hot mulled wine—*deux vins chauds*—and we commenced to catch up. As the pungent wine rolled through me—sleepless and jetlagged—I started wanting her again.

When lunch wrapped up I asked why I had never heard from her. She got a pained look and said, "I guess I thought it would be kinder if I just sort of faded away." As I tripped down the frigid sidewalks of Paris Vivienne's haunting voice followed me. I doubted she was as sorry as I was that she simply faded away.

Viv and I spent several days together in the city of love working my case. Then one afternoon in the chilly magnificence of the *Sacré Coeur*, the big white church atop Montmartre, she began to cry. I asked what was wrong. No reply. It wasn't until the next evening when we were toasting the apparent completion of my case that Vivienne proposed another toast—to her divorce. Her ex had taken up with a man. "It hurts," she whispered. I tried to comfort and reassure her. And then, as they say, one thing led to another.

I paddle into position along the south side of Flat Island. Kula and I wait. When a set rolls in I let the first wave go by and then paddle for the second. Kula pops up as I rise and swing the longboard to the left, steering clear of the coral heads in the shallows near the island. When the wave finally fizzles, I plop back down on the deck and give Kula a pat, "Atta boy!" The golden barks. He's stoked.

As we wait for another set my thoughts return to Vivienne. *Pregnant.* Friends of mine who've had babies say it spun their lives into a different orbit. They got little sleep and walked around like zombies. They had close to zero time for anything but the baby. Changing diapers, nursing and feedings, stacks of infant laundry, pediatrician appointments, and so on. Plus, all the stuff they had to buy: car seats, strollers, high chairs, cribs, baby gadgets and toys, baby-proofing supplies—and worst of all—a minivan! I look at my four-legged companion on the surfboard deck in front of me and say, "Kula, my friend, our lives are about to change."

He glances back at me and actually smiles. He has no idea.

Before it can all sink in, I see another wave on the horizon and we take it. Paddling back to the line-up after the ride I recall how, since Paris, Vivienne and I have bonded and worked through every obstacle. I'm reassured. We will figure out the baby thing—just like my friends figured it out. They survived. We will too.

Friday morning in my office I receive a text from pet detective Maile Barnes: "Looking forward to spending quality time with Kula next weekend," Maile says.

Maile and I don't talk much anymore since she married Frank Fernandez, except about the golden retriever. Maile was fostering Kula until Frank brought Blitz, his Rottweiler, into her Mānoa cottage and the Rottie beefed with the golden. I removed Kula to Vivienne's home in Kailua. Maile wasn't happy. She misses Kula. So I'm letting her take him for a weekend when she house-sits in Lanikai—without Blitz.

I text back a thumbs up.

The text from Maile brings to mind again my old buddy in the homicide division at the Honolulu Police Department.

I have an idea how Fernandez could help me further with the case. He already referred Detective Nakamura in Investigative Services on the Kaua'i force, for which I'm grateful. Now I recall that Professor Strohmeyer mentioned the O'ahu serial murderer who went on a rampage years before the Barking Sands Strangler. The so-called Honolulu Strangler racked up a higher body count than the killer on Kaua'i and had O'ahu residents, especially women, on edge for months. Fernandez was lead detective on the case. So he must know something about tracking these kinds of criminals.

But will he help me? I give him a call.

"Hey, Frank, how about lunch at the Wharf today—on me?" The Wharf is a popular local fish and seafood eatery overlooking Honolulu Harbor.

"The Wharf?" he asks in his gravelly voice. "What's this about, Kai?" The big man is instantly suspicious. I don't blame him.

"The Wharf is your favorite lunch spot, right?"

"Yeah, so what?" Is Fernandez in one of his foul moods? I better tread lightly.

"Got a favor, Frank. Well, a proposition, really. You tell me a little about the Honolulu Strangler and I buy you an *ahi* sandwich and a beer. Won't take but thirty minutes. What do you say?"

"Let me look at my calendar."

"Sure, Frank. Take your time." I hold on through silence while Fernandez decides whether or not he wants to bother.

Almost a minute later he asks: "Fries coming with that *ahi* sandwich?"

"Sure, Frank." I think I've got him. "French fries, *ahi,* and a beer—the whole tamale, all on me."

"Well, okay," he says, now in a sweeter mood. "See you there at noon." He hangs up.

The morning goes by and a little before noon I head over to the Wharf. When I arrive the pale November sun reflects in Honolulu Harbor like Kula's yellow tennis ball. I take a booth overlooking the water. The spar-varnished table could have been yanked from a ship's galley. The Wharf's ambience is nautical and seafaring—fishnets, a pilot wheel, lanyards, a captain's chair, and lifebuoys. A waitress in a sailor suit stops by and asks if I'm alone. I tell her I'm expecting someone. She leaves two menus.

At ten minutes after noon—about the wait I expect from Fernandez—the big man lumbers in, his huge frame filling the doorway. Even seeing him at this distance reminds me, if I need reminding, you don't want to mess with Frank Fernandez. Frank can be a grizzly bear or a teddy bear, depending on his mood. From his drawn face and bloodshot eyes, I don't know what to expect today. And I wonder how he's getting on with Maile. But he starts off friendly.

"Howzit, Kai?" He stretches out his huge mitt, we shake, and then he lowers himself into the booth.

"I'm fine." I discreetly dodge the incoming wave of his spicy aftershave. "And you?"

"Okay," Frank replies half-heartedly in his gruff voice. "So, you wanna know about serial killers?"

"Right," I reply. "You know already I'm working for the mother of one of the victims of the Barking Sands Strangler on Kaua'i. Thanks again, by the way, for the KPD referral. I doubt Detective Nakamura would have let me in the door without you putting in a word."

"No problem," the big man replies.

I shake my head. "I tried to say no to Mrs. Reece in every way I could, but I got the cold case anyway."

"Cold?" Fernandez raises his brows. *"Ice cold."*

"You got that right. I'm making some progress but anything you can tell me about tracking your Honolulu Strangler might help."

"Okay, let's talk about it," Frank says. "But it looks like we're going to order lunch first."

Frank's right. The female sailor is back and I quickly scan the menu. Frank doesn't bother. He knows what he wants. I order a Wharf burger.

The waitress departs and returns before long with Frank's beer. He gets right into it, sipping the foam off the head.

"Back in the mid-1980s," Fernandez begins, "the serial killer known as the Honolulu Strangler murdered five women in their late teens to mid-thirties. The women were raped and strangled and found in remote places with their hands tied behind them and unclothed from the waist down. I led the task force that tracked the killer. We actually caught the guy, but because of a frightened witness and lack of evidence he walked."

"Ugh!"

"To this day, he has not been charged. No one has."

"Some say the same thing happened with the Barking Sands Strangler."

Fernandez nods. "Today we have a Rapid DNA Machine that can give us results in ninety minutes. Back then, there was no such thing. This case happened before DNA was even used much in criminal investigations. If DNA was used at all, it took weeks to get results."

We're interrupted again by our sweetheart sailor with two oval platters bearing Fernandez's *ahi* and my burger.

"How about some ketchup?" Frank asks her, gazing at his golden-brown fries.

"Sure. Anything else?" She studies his bulldog face and he waves her off.

Before long she's back with the ketchup and Fernandez is on a roll, describing how he went about tracking the Honolulu Strangler.

"We looked at the killer's MO, from luring and restraining his victim to the way he actually murdered them and left his signature—the ritual the killer does that isn't necessary to the crime itself. As I'm sure you know, Kai, determining the signature and the MO are both aspects of profiling."

"The Barking Sands Strangler had his own signature," I reply. "A simple line drawing of a wave burned with a cigarette on the victim."

"I remember that wave," Fernandez says. He takes a bite of his seared *ahi* and then tells me about three databases his team used to track the killer: VICAP, the FBI's Violent Criminal Apprehension Program system providing patterns that link separate homicides; CODIS, the Combined DNA Index System, also FBI-administered, providing forensic profiles of convicted felons; and NCIC, the National Crime Information Center, distributing more data interlinked to federal, tribal, state, and local agencies and offices.

"You had access to all three databases and you still couldn't nail the guy?"

"Like I said, we caught him." Fernandez puts down his sandwich. "We just couldn't indict and convict him. We got no help from witnesses and our evidence was strong enough for HPD but not strong enough for the prosecuting attorney."

"They didn't have much better luck on Kaua'i, like I said. Some speculated that KPD was ill-equipped to handle a serial killing back then."

"Here's the problem," Frank continues. "In Hawai'i, unlike many states on the mainland, there is no state police force with an academy—no real-life *Hawaii Five-0*—where recruits from all islands receive uniform and professional training. It's up to each island to train their own. So in some cases you have the blind leading the blind."

"Hmmm." Since HPD couldn't nail the Honolulu Strangler, I wonder if Kaua'i police really did much worse with their strangler.

Frank shakes his head. "The Kaua'i force has made great strides in the last two decades. They're understaffed—what else is new?—but they're a better outfit than they were back then."

"I hear ya. Would Nakamura have been on the force two decades ago?"

Fernandez shrugs. "By the way, did Ellen give you anything?"

"Not directly. But she referred me to a retired officer who did. Ernie Hong told me how the Strangler case went down and he gave me mugshots of the top six suspects."

"I know Ernie!" Fernandez smiles. "Did he tell you he was on *Hawaii Five-0*?" Then he clarifies: "I mean the original *Five-*

0, not the reboot."

"Yeah, he mentioned it. Good-lookin' guy, even at his age."

"I'm sure you got more from Ernie than you would have from anybody on the force."

"I'm interviewing the first man on the mugshot list Ernie gave me on Sunday at Halawa. He's the guy some people think did it: Theron Walter."

The tab for lunch comes and Fernandez rises. "Good luck at Halawa. Getting an inmate to sing takes skill."

As Frank is about head for the door I say dryly, "I'll give it my best shot."

He looks down at me. "Don't be surprised if all you get are lies and denials."

twelve

Saturday morning Vivienne and I are sitting on the *lānai* reading the paper. Kula is curled up beside us. There's a short piece in the neighbor island section about Alana Newfield. She's been missing since Halloween—more than a week without a trace.

In other Kaua'i news incumbent prosecutor Buddy Kalaheo has prevailed in calling for a recount. The margin of victory had been small enough and allegations of irregularity convincing enough that election officials decided to begin the recount in the coming week, to include mail-in ballots that may not have been properly counted the first time around. I wonder if the election would have even been close except for the disappearance of Newfield's daughter, one of whose unintended consequences was immense publicity for the challenger.

The recount doesn't sound like good news for the prosecutor-elect. Or for his family. I remember the mask of desperation on his wife Margaret Anne's face and the look of bewilderment on the faces of their two younger daughters.

I ask Viv how she's feeling.

"Terrific," she replies. "I've come up with three girls' names."

"Girls names?"

"For the baby." She's ahead of me again.

"How do you like Camille or Madeleine or Bridgette?"

"If you like them, they're fine with me."

She pauses and gives me a look. "We have to hit on one we *both* really like. And boys' names too."

"Couldn't we just wait until we find out—girl or boy?"

"We could. But anticipation is part of the fun."

"Yeah, I see what you mean." I suddenly remember that it's time to clear out of my Waikīkī bachelor pad. My solo days at the Edgewater are dwindling.

She gives me another look. "Maybe you're caught up in your case? Have you found anything yet that will put that poor mother's mind at ease?"

"A few small things. In the beginning, it's usually just bits and pieces. Down the road all the small stuff could eventually add up to something. Tomorrow I'm interviewing a suspect in Halawa Prison."

"On Sunday?"

"Visiting hours are on weekends only."

"Strange."

"Not when you think about it. Weekends are when people are usually off from work."

When Sunday comes I take the H-3 Freeway from the Windward side to Halawa Correctional Facility in Aiea, just shy of Aloha Stadium. On the way I recall what Frank Fernandez said I could expect from interviewing an inmate:

lies and denials.

Tucked in little valley beneath Aiea Ridge, Halawa must be the hottest spot on the island. It's sweltering. The correctional facility consists of a bunch of concrete slabs. The only architectural feature that lifts the eye is a single watchtower from which guards monitor inmates through darkened glass. It's not a cheery place. But, I guess, it's not supposed to be. The medium security facility housing inmates who have committed a felony (like my former client Barry Buckingham) is the largest correctional institution in the state. Overcrowding has led to shipping part of the prison population to private facilities on the mainland. Prisoners left behind are the lucky ones. At least they get to serve their time in Hawai'i and see family and friends in person. I doubt I'll receive the warm welcome they would.

I leave my cellphone—it's contraband—in my car and get signed in and cleared through security. Only visitors on the inmate's approved list are allowed, so I called ahead. My name was added to the list of inmate Theron Walter— whose criminal history includes kidnapping, sexual assault, attempted murder, drug offenses, and parole violations. And, of course, Walter was, and is still, on the top of KPD's Strangler list. The story goes that he committed the three murders and walked because investigators could not assemble a strong enough case.

After I'm cleared into the visiting room I sit across from Theron Walter, thick glass between us with a metal grate allowing us to hear one another. A small partition on either side of the glass offers minimal privacy. A dozen such booths line two opposite walls.

The now older Walter faintly resembles his mugshot, but with pasty prison skin and closer-clipped salt and pepper hair. Once a good-looking man, his dark brown eyes have become the color of mud. Worry lines roll like waves from temple to temple down his forehead. Walter must have a lot on his mind. His nose is bent, maybe from a prison fight? He wears a scraggly mustache that looks drunk and disorderly.

I ask him right off about the Barking Sands murders.

"It wasn't me!" Walter sings like a soprano, his high voice not what I expected from a hard-core felon. "Kaua'i police got it wrong. I had nothing to do with those murders."

"Why do you think they fingered you?"

"I happened to be out and they picked me up. For no good reason. I didn't know any of those women. I never even seen any of 'em."

"Didn't they say you were violating the terms of your parole?"

Walter shakes his head. "None of what they blame me for is my fault. The world made me the way I am. I'm just doing what I was programmed to do. But I get blamed."

"And the other assaults you're in here for?"

He shrugs. "Women come on to me. They ask for it. And I give it to 'em. And then they say they didn't want it! And who do the judges believe? *Them*."

I try to keep him talking. "So you never got a fair shake?"

"The whole damn system is stacked against me."

"If you didn't commit the Barking Sands murders, who did?" I rattle off the names of the other suspects.

"None of those guys."

"What's the word in Halawa?"

"Nobody in here knows the guy because he's never been inside. It's somebody outside—maybe still living on Kaua'i."

"His name?"

"If I knew it would be worth something, eh?"

"You have inside information? I'm all ears."

"I'll ask around," Walter replies. "I usually keep to myself. Some guys in here hate me for no good reason."

"Must be tough." As a sex offender, Walter would occupy the lowest rung in the prison hierarchy. I doubt he gets much respect.

"I don't want to die in prison," he says out of the blue.

"Why do you keep coming back?"

"I mean I don't want to get killed in here."

"Is there anything I could do for you on the outside?" I try to win his cooperation.

"You can put money in my account," he replies. "Up to $250 by cashier's check."

"Just get me a name or a lead or anything and I'll deposit in your account."

"Like I said," Walter replies, "I'll ask around."

"Aloha Theron." I rise from my chair. "Good luck."

Walking to my car I'm not believing much of what the jailbird has said. No surprise. Like Fernandez predicted, Walter takes no responsibility for anything he's done. None of it is his fault. He blames his crimes on his circumstances and his victims. Not to say his young life ever gave him much of a chance. He could have grown up around abuse and violence. I should feel sorry for him. Maybe I could, if I hadn't seen so many victims of guys like him.

After returning from Halawa I take my longboard to Kakaʻako Waterfront Park. The park is best known for an edgy body-surfing spot near the Honolulu Harbor channel called Point Panic, where green barrels thunder into a rock seawall. Body surfers milk each curl to its last drop, then pull out a split second before colliding with the wall. I guess that's why they call the spot Point Panic. Definitely not for surfboards.

I walk *ewa* of Point Panic to one of my favorite town spots, a break friendly to longboard riders called Flies. Though on the edge of the Paradise College campus, it's seldom crowded like Waikīkī. Only two surfers out today. Riding a few waves might help me clear the cobwebs after my prison visit and meditate on the case. Sherlock Holmes had his pipe; I have my surfboard.

I grab my board, climb down the stairs to the water, say my mantra and paddle out. The swell is running about chest high, producing a consistent but mushy right. I paddle into position and look out to sea. In the distance I see a set coming. The two other surfers paddle for it. When the first shoulder-high roller reaches the pair, both riders drop in. I maneuver into the spot they leave behind. A second wave rolls in. I swing my board around and stroke until I feel the rush of water under me. My board takes on the steep pitch of the wave. A spritzer of saltwater flies over the nose. I pop up, turn right, and stay just in front of the curling lip.

Ho! I'm really moving.

After the wave breaks and my board glides to a stop I chug back into the lineup. I ride another when a new set rolls in. Then there's a lull.

Between sets I think about Theron Walter's claim that the

Barking Sands Strangler is not among KPD's list of six. Walter thinks the killer has been hidden in plain sight on Kaua'i, living two distinctly separate lives. People I've interviewed on opposite sides of the law—inmate Walter and Prosecutor-elect Newfield—believe the same thing.

Are they right? Could the Barking Sands Strangler be alive and well on the Garden Isle? By scratching the surface I've already turned up two names from the past—Josh and Mitch—that could fit. And another West Side man that Ernie Hong mentioned. And the kayak rental proprietor in Hanalei named Boz who I'll look up next time on the island.

Not exactly a breakthrough. But something.

Sunday evening Vivienne and I are in bed when her phone rings. It's after ten. A little late for a call?

"Oh, *hello.*" Vivienne answers. I know from her tone who's on the other end.

She listens to Jeremy's plaintive voice. I can hear him too, barely.

"I'm so sorry." Viv says sympathetically. "That must be dreadful for you. What's *wrong* with that man?"

I guess they're talking about her ex's new partner. Jeremy keeps talking. More problems?

Viv eventually steers the conversation away from him and his worries. "How is Sadie?" That's their Labrador retriever—or was their Labrador until Vivienne lost her in the divorce. Now she belongs to Jeremy.

Should I get worked up about my girlfriend—my pregnant girlfriend—talking to her ex? She says she's just trying to help an old friend through rough times. But Jeremy calls often.

Too often for me. Viv dropped out of my life to marry this guy. Then he left her for another relationship—but he keeps clinging to her. Why? My response to him is simple: You made your choice, now live with it. Let us be.

I don't want to tell Vivienne what to do. I don't want to be a dictator. But I've had enough. It's not like she and her ex have children. Well, there's Sadie. But they seldom talk about the Labrador. It's always about Jeremy.

Everybody's got problems.

Their conversation goes on. By the time she's finally off the phone I'm irked.

She sees the look in my eyes and says, "You talk to Maile." She's referring to the pet detective, my former girlfriend. "And I don't give it a thought."

"Maile and I talk about Kula," I reply. "But she hardly ever calls and never at this hour."

"I don't care when she calls or what you two talk about," Viv says. "Every little thing doesn't set me off."

I shrug.

"Kai, we're having a baby." She sounds tender now. "I love you. I even love your shark tattoo." She smiles and points to the little pink welts on my bare chest.

I turn out the light. She snuggles next to me.

"You okay?" she whispers.

"Yeah, I'm okay," I say. But I still don't like her ex.

thirteen

First thing on Monday I get a call from Seattle PI Kitty Stockwell. Kitty has followed Alana Newfield's trail into Emerald City nightlife and discovered that the Kaua'i County Prosecutor-elect's daughter worked in strip clubs while attending Saint Ursula College, most recently under the name Sindee Sparks. Alana, a.k.a. Sindee, had also done freelance work for escort services.

Then Kitty drops another bomb. "Alana's ex-boyfriend," she says, "is a pimp."

"So why did Alana leave Saint Ursula?"

"She was expelled," Kitty explains in her larger-than-life voice.

"Expelled?"

"Yes, after arrest for prostitution."

"Could Alana have gone freelance on Kaua'i when she returned home to her parents?"

"Possible. These days all she'd need is an internet hookup," Kitty replies. "But that's your territory, Kai."

"My territory?"

"I mean it's in your islands. Not in my Seattle," she says.

"I'll email you court documents concerning her arrest and hearing. She got probation, by the way. Her first offense. I'll attach a couple of stories from the Seattle paper about the sting operation that caught her."

"Thanks, Kitty," I say. "Send me your invoice."

"My invoice will come with the docs," she replies. "And next time, Kai, it's a free trip to Paradise."

"No worries." I laugh. "When my big Detroit case comes through—the sky's the limit."

"I'll hold you to it, *Mr. Surfing Detective.*"

Kitty's poking fun at my agency's name is nothing new. When I first opened for business, hardly a week went by without a crank call. Celebrity seekers back then, bleary-eyed from reruns of the old *Hawaii Five-0,* phoned my office for Jack Lord, a.k.a. Captain Steve McGarrett. *Go figure.* I look nothing like Lord, nor from the reruns I've seen did he ever surf. I also got calls for *Magnum P.I.* Late one night a crazed woman whispered into my phone a breathy, *"Thomas Magnum?"* Before I could break the news that her heartthrob Tom Selleck had left the islands, she hung up. I couldn't complain. At least my phone was ringing. Back then crank calls were better than silence.

After talking with Kitty Stockwell I wonder again if Newfield knew his daughter had been arrested in Seattle. And if he knew the charges. He didn't tell me. Did he tell Kaua'i police? I guess there's ample reason not to reveal this potentially embarrassing information about one's own child. But wouldn't Newfield, as an attorney and a prosecutor-elect, know such information might help law enforcement find his daughter? Then there's Newfield's own reputation, especially while campaigning for office.

My thoughts are interrupted by another call, this one from attorney Oscar Chang at the law offices of Ossendorfer, Noboru, and Chang. Is this the call I've been waiting for? The big case for the high-profile attorney?

"Matt wants to reassure you, Kai," Chang says, "that the Detroit case is on. Just a few preliminaries before we get started."

"No worries," I say, wondering what he means.

"Our client wants to know about everyone under contract with the firm who will be working on the case . . . their experience and qualifications. That sort of thing. Automakers have to be so careful these days."

"Understood."

"We have no doubt about you, Kai. But we have to present something in writing to Detroit within a day or so. Could you send us a resumé that details your education, training, license, and your years and experience on the job? Successful cases, court testimonies for your clients, that sort of thing."

"No problem. I'll get something over to you shortly."

"Excellent. We don't expect this today. Tomorrow would be fine."

Chang hangs up.

I have no such document. No one has ever asked for it. My formal education and training are sketchy. I'll have to go into my files and summarize a few of my more notable cases and provide a list of court depositions. This kind of meaningless paperwork is exactly the type of thing I hate. But to play in the big league, I figure, you've got to play by their rules.

I could ask Vivienne for help. In her professional circles

these kinds of requests are routine. But to ask her would call attention to the gap between a Ph.D. and a college dropout. Though I graduated from Flintridge Prep's college AP program, during my first year at university in San Diego I surfed myself right out of school. Since then I've earned my credentials on the job. And that's more difficult to document than degrees and certificates and honors and awards.

There are reasons why I didn't finish college. Or, truth be told, why I barely got through my first year. After my mother and father's plane crash I was alone in the world, except for my dog Pono. The Kealoha family on the North Shore, whose matriarch was my mother's sister, Auntie Mae, welcomed Pono and me into their *ohana* and treated us as their own. Accustomed to the prep school atmosphere of hallowed Punahou—alma mater of a former U.S. President—I didn't get on well at the large public school my Kealoha cousins attended. My grades fell. Through lengthy family negotiations I was too young to understand, I was relocated to my uncle Orson Cooke's home in Pasadena, California, and attended Flintridge Prep with my cousin Matthew.

On weekends Matthew and I haunted our favorite So Cal surf spots and after graduating we both trekked south to California Surfside College, perched on the cliffs of Point Loma. Cal Surf, as we wave-crazed students called it, boasted four of the best breaks in San Diego. I clocked more hours in the water than in the classroom. And got kicked out. I could have returned after my probation, but I never did.

Uncle Orson had generously bankrolled my education. But I couldn't in good conscience take any more of his money. I kick myself today for that decision, but I just wanted to come home to the islands. I had no funds to get there or to live on once I did. So when an Army recruiter promised me a surf instructor gig for R & R troops at Fort DeRussy in Waikīkī I signed on—then spent my entire tour in the infantry. When finally discharged I landed a job as an assistant claims adjuster at Acme Casualty where cousin Matthew, his bachelor's degree in hand, was already a management trainee. Acme is the same firm that these days hires me to investigate insurance fraud in the islands.

Though I never finished college, claims work taught me more about human nature than I could have learned in any psychology course. I witnessed more half-truths, deception, scams, and outright lies than I care to remember. This glimpse into the darker side prepared me—better than any classroom—for my later occupation. That's how I earned my credentials. On the job. And in my line of work, street smarts trump degrees and honors and awards every time.

After the phone call from Oscar Chang I spend the rest of the day in my office pouring over my files, sneezing from the dust and mold on yellowed paper, and cursing the demand for documentation. I could always say no. But that might also mean no more business from Ossendorfer.

Later that Monday I receive a call from Zanie Moon, Tommy's new girlfriend. She's a tiny Filipino woman with delicate features and shimmering black hair. I don't know her well. I met her only once at Tommy's gig at a backwater hotel called the Waikīkī Seacrest. Zanie sings with his trio. She has a vibrant contralto voice and a degree in music.

"Kai," Zanie says in a soft but anxious tone, "I'm worried

about Tommy."

"What's wrong?" I ask, but think I know.

"Last night at the Seacrest we were in the middle of "Lush Life," and I was singing about living each day as if it were the last, when Tommy dropped his head on the keys."

"Hmmm."

"Eugene and Jonny and I didn't know what to do." She's referring to bassist Eugene Pham and drummer Jonny LeBaron.

"How long was Tommy out?"

"Not long. He sat up and started playing again like nothing happened. We went along, figuring the audience might think it was a gag."

"It was no gag."

"I know," she replies. "After the gig I tried to talk to him. No go."

"Tommy has a mind of his own."

"I love him for it," she says. "But he can be difficult."

"I hear ya."

"Can you try? Can you talk to him?"

"I did. Last time we had dinner at Ah Fook. I got the same response."

"Please try again."

When Zanie hangs up I punch in Tommy's number and get his voicemail. "Hey Tommy," I say, "would you give me a call? Got a question for you."

That's sounds vague enough. I figure he'll call back shortly, unless he already suspects Zanie has worked on me.

I don't hear from Tommy that day or the next.

It's late afternoon on Tuesday before I can cobble together the resumé requested by Ossendorfer, Noboru, and Chang. Worrying that an email might lose my digital copy somewhere up in the cloud, I walk a hard copy to the law firm's nearby Bishop Street office. Strolling in the cooling air does me good after being cooped up for hours. But I've wasted an entire day on paperwork. As I return on foot to Maunakea Street I'm thinking: I would do this for no one but Matt Ossendorfer.

That evening I'm cruising over the Pali Highway toward Kailua when I hear on the radio that a prison brawl at Halawa this morning left one inmate dead. His name is being withheld pending notification of next of kin. While other prisoners had minor injuries, only one was killed. Could Theron Walter be the lone victim? Was Walter taken out only a few days after I visited him because he asked too many questions about the Strangler?

Wednesday I'm back at the main branch of the state library on Punchbowl Street in the Hawaiʻi Room looking at everything I can find on the six active persons of interest on the Barking Sands list: Stephen "Stubby" Kahale, Korgan Lee, Joel Merryweather, Michael Julio Rabino, Theron Walter, and the unidentified man in the police sketch. Despite Walter's belief that the Strangler is not on this list, I want to check out every prospect in the event I can find something that law enforcement may have missed. Since the murders date back twenty years, most of what I discover is on microfilm. But I also consult a few hardcopy articles and stories from the library's files in newsprint.

This is what I find: Stephen "Stubby" Kahale is locked up

in Texas, Korgan Lee is on parole on the Garden Isle, Joel Merryweather's last known address was Sparks, Nevada; Michael Julio Rabino was knifed to death in a late-night scuffle in Honolulu's Chinatown; Theron Walter I of course recently interviewed in Halawa Prison; and the unidentified man in the sketch appears to have slipped off the face of the earth. With Rabino's death the active list is now whittled down to five: four named persons and one unnamed for whom there is no account.

I dig further into persons known and unknown for the better part of a day. I don't find anything unique or telling about any of the five. And I begin to agree with Walter that the Barking Sands Strangler, unless he's the man in the police sketch, may never have been among those on the list. He's someone who has a perfect cover. He's someone who lives above suspicion—even after all these years.

Thursday morning I drive Vivienne to the airport for her flight to San Francisco. She's speaking on French writer George Sand at a conference in Berkeley. Viv is scheduled to return Tuesday evening. Driving back to my office I hear on the radio that Tuesday's victim at Halawa Prison was in fact Theron Walter. Good thing I got to him before he died. But I wonder again if my asking him to inquire about the Strangler jinxed him. Or was it because, as a sex offender, he was so low on the prison pecking order he got pecked to death?

I'm about to reserve a flight to Kaua'i, since Maile Barnes will be taking Kula for the weekend, when I get a call from the pet detective herself.

"Hey, Kai. I'm on Kaua'i working a stolen dog case and

may not return to O'ahu on time Friday to pick up Kula for my housesitting gig in Lanikai."

"You're on Kaua'i?" I reply. "I've got a case there too."

"Really? Say, if I can't return in time, could you take Kula to Lanikai for me until I get there, hopefully later on Friday? I'll call the Van Ormes and tell them you'll be holding down the fort until I arrive."

"I can't, Maile. Like I said, I've got a case on Kaua'i too and I'm about to book a flight back tomorrow. Plus, I have another big gig about to start with Matt Ossendorfer."

"You've got to do this for me, Kai. I can't leave this case."

"Why not ask Frank?"

"Frank can't leave Blitz alone and Blitz can't come to this fancy home, especial with Kula there."

"True, the Rottweiler and Kula don't get along. Well, Kula is fine with any dog. But Blitz is aggressive."

"Even if he could leave Blitz behind, Frank's not the right person for this job. He's a great cop. He's a great guy. But he's not much of a housekeeper. He would be like a bull in a china shop. And if you add Blitz . . . well, forget about it."

"Gotta agree with you there."

"When you needed me, Kai, remember how I came through for you? You wouldn't even have Kula without me. I recovered him for you."

She's right. We flew to Maui together and she liberated him from an oceanfront home in Lahaina. A woman named Varda had bought him—and may or may not have known Kula had been stolen.

"Kai? Can I count on you?" Maile's sounding desperate now. "I'll pass along the hundred bucks a day I get for the

Lanikai gig, just for holding my spot until I return."

"When will you return from Kaua'i?" I know I'm licked, but I stall.

"Best case, Friday afternoon. Then you're off the hook. And I'll give you the C-note for just a few hours of hanging out."

"And worst case?"

"You might have to drive the Van Ormes to the airport. I always do that for them. They'll let you drive their Tesla."

"Swell," I reply, a little testy.

"You just drop them at the airport and then return the Tesla home to their garage. Then I should be back soon after to relieve you."

"And if you're later? Say, if you don't get home Friday night?"

"You need me to watch Kula, Kai, or you can't go to Kaua'i yourself, right?"

"How'd you know?"

"You already told me Vivienne would be on the mainland."

I'm feeling somewhat ambushed. "Okay."

"Mahalo, Kai! I really appreciate it." Maile gives me directions to the Van Ormes' and promises to keep me posted on her whereabouts.

"See you on Friday," I say.

Maile hesitates. "Uh, I'll do my best."

fourteen

On Friday I spend the day in my office and then head home early to beat the afternoon Pali commute. I'm barely in the door when I get a call from Maile.

"Kai, I'm still on Kaua'i. I'll be late to the Van Ormes."

"I'll cover it," I say, "like we agreed."

"Could you go now?"

"Sure, I'm on my way."

I put Kula in my car and drive into Lanikai—little more than a mile from Vivienne's Kailua home.

I believe through my PI work I've driven every road on this island. I'm wrong. I've never been on the winding private lane at the end of Lanikai that leads to this hilltop estate. I climb until I can see those iconic twin islands—the Mokuluas or Mokes—that have replaced Diamond Head as the most familiar tourist-brochure image of the Hawaiian Islands. I pull up to a copper-patinaed gate depicting frolicking dolphins and enter the code Maile has given me. The gate swings open to a mammoth banyan and grass-pave driveway circling it. Beyond the banyan the sprawling home—roof covered with solar panels—overlooks those cozy twin islands on the turquoise sea.

I park and am greeted by a trim silver-haired man who's no doubt older than he looks. Hawai'i keeps *kupuna*—elders—looking young. Especially elders with money. I explain to Mr. Van Orme that I'm spelling for Maile until she arrives later this evening. He glances at my ancient Impala and looks skeptical. The teal paint is original but more than a half-century old. I assure him Maile will be along shortly. Mrs. Van Orme soon joins us. She's also silver and well-kept like her husband and also looks skeptical.

Then I let the retriever out of the car. Kula prances up to the couple, his golden coat glowing in the afternoon sun. Their skepticism melts away. They hug and baby talk him like I'm not there. They forget themselves. Kula has that effect on people. I'm now in the Van Ormes' good graces. Turns out they once had a golden retriever. Kula's arrival brings back warm memories.

Soon Mr. Van Orme produces their luggage. I help him load it in their Tesla, he shows me how to drive the electric car—powered, he explains, by the sun—and we're off. On the way, he lectures me on climate change, renewable energy, and a sustainable future for the islands. He's a retired professor and his remarks easily fill the twenty-five-minute ride to the airport.

I return to Kula resting comfortably in their hilltop estate above Lanikai. I watch a pair of yellow kayaks paddling to the twin islands land on the sandy beach of the northern Moke.

My cellphone rings. It's Maile.

"Coming to relieve me?" I ask.

She doesn't answer. She tells me more about her case. "You

see, Kai, Brittanie was the live-in caretaker of the Skye terrier named Precious owned by my client, Ian Boz. Brittanie stole the dog from Boz, for reasons he didn't tell me."

"The name Boz sounds familiar."

"He lives in Princeville and owns a watersport rental business in Hanalei."

"*Bingo.* I want to meet your client."

"Why?" Maile asks.

"It's a longshot, but he might be connected to the Barking Sands case."

"Good. Maybe we can help each other."

"I'm for that," I say. "But when are you getting here?"

Maile continues her story. "So, Brittanie steals Precious back on Halloween Day."

"That's when Alana Newfield went missing."

"Yes, I remember. Anyway, since Halloween Brittanie has been on the lam. Boz needs the Skye terrier back before his absent wife returns in a few days. It's her dog. And she apparently has money. I suspect she underwrites Boz's business and his upscale lifestyle."

"Oh, so he *really* needs that dog back!"

"Exactly. After searching the Garden Isle, I finally located Brittanie and Precious today, but just as the two were boarding a Hawaiian Airlines flight to Los Angeles. I'm now boarding a United flight to LA."

"You're flying to LA? You said you'd relieve me tonight."

"I wish I could, Kai. I really do."

I'm speechless.

Maile keeps going. "I doubt my client's version of events. Brittanie is twenty-one. And Boz appears to be in his forties.

I suspect there was more to their relationship while his wife was away than Boz is telling me. Mrs. Elizabeth Boz is returning from a cooking course in Italy and her husband is desperate to get her dog back before she arrives."

"I'm useless to my Kauaʻi investigation," I say, "sidetracked by your pet-theft case."

"I'll hook you up with Boz. What you see now as a detour, Kai, may break your case wide open."

"Boz a longshot—like I said."

"The airplane is pushing back," she replies. "Gotta go!"

Auwe! Looks like I'm stuck in Lanikai.

I'm bummed. But things could be worse. I attach Kula's leash and walk him down to the beach. Fact is, I haven't been here in years.

The little side street to the beach is slammed on both sides with rental cars. Barely one lane is passable. And when the golden boy leads me down the sandy access to the water, I'm staggered by what I see. Every grain of sand appears to be covered by glistening bodies. We step gingerly around beach mats, chairs, umbrellas, coolers, tents, and all that tanning flesh.

I remember coming to Lanikai when I was younger, before the H-3 Freeway was blasted through the Koʻolaus. In those days the little pristine beach was a well-kept secret. Windward folks came here. And a few Marines from the nearby base. But seldom tourists. There were no amenities—still aren't. No toilets, no showers, no picnic tables, no off-street parking. Nothing. Just a secluded ribbon of white sand and turquoise sea with those magical twin islands offshore.

Then Dr. Beach named Lanikai the best beach of the year.

Before long tour buses and rental cars brought Waikīkī to the Windward side. The formerly deserted streets of the little hamlet clogged. Unlicensed vacation rentals sprouted like poison mushrooms. Lanikai became a tourist destination. Residents complained, but little changed. The hordes kept coming.

I tiptoe around the glinting masses, keeping Kula on leash. Even without the crowds there's not much sand. Erosion and sea-level rise have shrunk the once broad sweep of sand to less than half its former glory. Kula doesn't mind. His sun-soaked splendor elicits its usual *oohs* and *ahs*. The boy gives beachgoers his melting brown-eyed retriever gaze that says, "How can you resist me?" Truth is, they can't. They utter words like: "I love your dog!" "Hey handsome!" (to him, not to me) "Can I pet your pup?"

And so it goes. Kula laps it up. He loves adoration. He would hang out for human strokes all day if I didn't drag him away.

Reminds me of the first time I laid eyes on Kula. Not in person. On a television screen. I was working for the dog's master at the time, as I mentioned, who's currently serving a life sentence at Halawa. Kula had been stolen from Barry Buckingham and his daughter, Lehua. He hired me to find the dog. Buckingham played a video showing the golden retriever careering down the face of a sizable wave at Mākaha—Kula crouched on the nose of a longboard piloted by Lehua. The narrator from a local TV news program referred to him as the famous Hawaiian surfing dog. I was impressed.

Down on the shore I toss a tennis ball into the water and the golden boy dashes after it. Kula chugs into the surf. He's having a blast. Same drill as on Kailua Beach.

Kailua is the beach where I first traced Kula. I arrived early one morning when the blue bay was all but invisible in the predawn darkness. My eyes kept returning to the Lanikai boat ramp—situated between Kailua and Lanikai—the exact spot where Lehua had last seen Kula. Once the sun rose I showed Kula's photo around. Later I posted flyers offering a large reward in every nearby neighbourhood. And I put ads in both Honolulu subscription newspapers of the day. No luck. Not until Maile and I found him in an oceanfront villa in Lahaina on the island of Maui.

Kula returns dripping wet with the tennis ball and I toss it again into the surf. He dashes in and paddles toward the prize. Once we recovered and returned the golden retriever to Oʻahu, his master was inexplicably gone. Turns out Buckingham had set sail to a remote Pacific island to avoid the raft of felony charges, including murder, that eventually landed him at Halawa. His daughter and estranged wife did manage to flee him, and potential legal problems, but not before dropping by my office and leaving Kula with me—*forever*. Never mind that the Waikīkī Edgewater didn't allow pets. Maile adopted Kula and gave him a good home until Frank and Blitz arrived. That's when I brought Kula to Vivienne's. It didn't all go smoothly. But you'd never believe such a fabulous dog could come from such a dreadful crook.

When I finally pull out his leash signaling it's time go, Kula swims to a nearby exposed reef, plants himself on it, and looks back at me with the most defiance such a malleable breed can muster. I wade in up to my hips and attach his leash. He knows the game is up. Soon we're hiking up the beach

access, Kula sandy and soaked and calm. I glance back at those
gorgeous twin islands, a few puffy clouds scudding over them
in the azure sky. That last look redeems the day.

Back at the Van Ormes' hilltop estate I hear nothing from
Maile—no wonder—on an overnight flight from Līhu‘e to
Los Angeles.

After dinner that evening I call Vivienne in Berkeley. I
explain I'm spelling for Maile in Lanikai.

"You must be the world's best ex-boyfriend." It's soothing
to hear Viv's lovely voice, but there's an edge to it. She's never
shown a hint of jealously about Maile.

"Long story," I say. "The short version is I got roped into
it."

"I'm sure I don't need to hear the long version."

"How are you feeling?" I wonder if her pregnancy has her
on edge.

"Not nauseous today," she says. "And I'm enjoying seeing
colleagues and old friends."

"Anybody I know?"

"Well, I did run into Jeremy."

"Did his partner come along?"

"No, Jeremy's alone."

I could get worked up about this unpleasant surprise—my
girlfriend and her ex together at Berkeley—but I take the
high ground. "I'm sure he's glad you're there."

"Thanks, darling. I'm happy you understand."

I'm proud of myself. No point in showing any further
jealousy about Jeremy. It's not going to stop her anyway. I
have to believe she's sincere when she says she considers him
an old friend. And I have to admire that she's been able to get

over his betrayal.

Then Viv asks, "How's your case coming?"

"Mrs. Reece was happy with my first report," I reply. "And I'm heading back to Kaua'i as soon as I get sprung from this housesitting gig—with a new lead."

"How did that come about?"

"Maile's client is very likely the same man I was told resembles a police sketch in the Strangler case."

"A happy coincidence?"

"Whatever comes of it, I'll be home by Tuesday night to pick you up at the airport."

"Looking forward," she says. And then: "Kai, you have nothing to worry about with Jeremy. He and I are long over as a couple. But I don't throw away old friends. That's not my style."

"I respect you for that," I say and carry the thought to bed.

fifteen

My phone's chime wakes me Saturday morning before seven. It's a text from Mrs. Reece: "Did you see the news from Kaua'i in this morning's paper? Just what I feared."

I fetch the Van Ormes' newspaper and turn to the neighbor island section. In the left column about halfway down:

BODY OF MISSING KAUA'I WOMAN FOUND

"Alana Newfield, daughter of Kaua'i County Prosecutor-elect Janson Newfield III, was found dead in an as-yet undisclosed location on the Garden Isle. She had been missing since Halloween Night. No other information is being released at this time pending further investigation by Kaua'i Police."

I find Janson Newfield's number in my phone, pause a moment, and decide that even though I didn't warm to the man, this is the right thing to do.

I call Newfield and get his voicemail, not surprising considering the early hour.

"Hello, Mr. Newfield. It's Kai Cooke. Please accept my sincere condolences for your loss. My thoughts are with you and your family. Anything I can do, please let me know."

Within a couple of minutes my phone rings.

"This is the work of the Strangler." It's Newfield. "I guarantee you. He is back. And he has struck at me and my family because I have dared to proclaim I will find him and prosecute him."

"Was there evidence of the Strangler?"

"I am not at liberty to provide details at this time, but soon you will see. He's back."

The minute Newfield hangs up I text Maile: "Big developments on Kaua'i. I have to return immediately. When can you relieve me?"

I wait. No reply.

I assume she's in the thick of her pursuit of the young woman named Brittanie who stole the Skye terrier. Until I hear from Maile I'm stuck. There's no point in booking a flight to Līhu'e until I know when she's returning. And that could be another day.

I gaze from the Van Ormes' *lānai* upon the tranquil waters of Lanikai with one jarring thought: another young woman has been murdered on Kaua'i. I've got to think through my next move, even though delayed until Maile's return. And I know the best way to get my thoughts flowing.

I search the Van Ormes' carriage house and find a stand-up paddle board that's long enough to function as a tandem board for Kula and me. I put Kula on leash and walk him and the board to the beach.

Not so many people colonizing the sand this early on

Saturday morning. I plop down the board, wax up, and Kula hops on. I say my mantra and paddle straight out toward the islands, navigating carefully around shallow inside reefs. At low tide these reefs can rise up like razor blades and rip boards to shreds—not to mention board riders. The waves break far out here when the swell reaches at least six feet. Smaller rollers just bump over the outer reefs without cresting. So the swell we're looking for will be almost overhead.

I paddle into position north of the two islands. Out on the horizon the blue sea meets the paler blue sky. We wait. I glance back to the distant shore at what looks tiny doll houses dotting Lanikai beach. I have a moment to think. When I'm out in the waves my head clears. I can sometimes see things in a new light.

Alana Newfield is dead. All the facts haven't been made public yet, but her father insists they point to a return of the Strangler. According to the Prosecutor-elect, after twenty years the Strangler has returned to target Newfield's own daughter. Could his shock over Alana's sudden death be affecting his reason? Dormant for two decades the serial killer suddenly strikes again? Even ten years, if we count Amity Johnson's murder as Newfield does, is a long time. I recall Professor Strohmeyer explaining that these killers do occasionally take long breaks. Is that likely in this case?

Out on the blue horizon a set is coming. The first wave approaches, building slowly. It's better than six feet. I swing the board around and start paddling. Kula crouches on the nose. I glance back. The wave forms into a steep wall and the board pitches down. Kula tenses. I feel a rush under us and I pop up. Kula balances, spreading his paws, as I trim the board.

The wave curls over my head. We glide down the face and I swing the nose to the right, trying to steer clear of the razor-sharp reefs. I muscle the board harder right and we shoot past the danger. Kula barks. *Stoked!* We live to catch another wave.

Lucky you live Hawai'i, as we say. I feel sorry for my landlocked friends who can surf only virtual waves. If just once in their lives they could paddle out and catch a real wave—feel the burn in their arms and the salt spray in their face—then they'd know. Sitting on their *'ōkole* in front of a screen is hardly the same thing.

After a few more rides I paddle in and we hike back to the Van Ormes' estate. We chill for the remainder of the day. That evening I receive a call from Straub Hospital. It's Tommy.

"Kai, I passed out last night at the Seacrest. I woke up and was fine, but Zanie already called an ambulance and I ended up at Straub."

"What's wrong with you?"

"Probably nothing. They're just doing tests. These vampires love my blood. See why I don't like hospitals? I just wanna get outta here."

"Yeah, but first you've got to get yourself checked to find out what's going on."

He doesn't respond.

"Hang on, Tommy. I'll come visit you."

"Don't bother, Kai. I'll be outta here in no time," he insists. Then: "Gotta go. They're poking me again!"

I hop in my car and drive over the Pali Highway to Straub Hospital. When I find Tommy's room my friend is being attended by several medical staff. He's hooked up to an IV and oxygen. His vital signs are blipping by on a nearby screen.

He looks pale. A nurse asks if I'm family. Tommy tells her I'm his only family. Well, besides his girlfriend. He confides to me that he doesn't really know when they'll spring him from the hospital. And then: "Kai, could you feed my two cats?"

"Sure, Tommy. Any way I can help."

After some discussion he manages to give me his apartment key and instructions.

Just before I go Tommy says, "Oh, I forgot to tell you something about Janson Newfield that you may want to know."

"You don't need to tell me now, Tommy," I say. "It can wait until you're feeling better."

He shrugs. "Maybe I better tell you now."

"Whatevahs."

"Come closer, Kai."

I walk right up next to his hospital bed.

Tommy speaks softly, almost in a whisper. "Long before his run for Kaua'i County Prosecutor, Newfield asked me— confidentially—if I knew any PIs on O'ahu who would track a Honolulu defendant's car. I didn't call you on that one, Kai."

"Why, Tommy? You know I can follow a car."

"I know. That wasn't the issue."

"What was?"

Just then Tommy's torch-singer girlfriend Zanie steps through the doorway of the patient's room, her shimmering black hair falling nearly to her waist. She gestures to me and I step toward her.

"How is he?" she whispers.

"I don't know," I reply softly. "Maybe a doc will fill you in."

"Did you call Tommy after we talked?" She peers into my

eyes.

"I left him a message. He didn't return my call until tonight."

"That man!" She utters under her breath and marches into the room.

I drive to Tommy's disordered apartment in Makiki. Charlie and Miles haven't been fed since yesterday and are all over me. I do what I've been asked to do. I even sit on Tommy's fur-infested couch and let both cats crawl over me. I've never owned a cat and don't know much about caring for them. But they seem to like me. Or maybe they're just lonely and hungry?

I fill their water and food dishes and make my way out, wondering why Tommy told me from his hospital bed about Newfield looking for a PI to follow a car on Oʻahu. My attorney friend left me up in the air.

sixteen

First thing on Sunday I check the morning paper. This time the story about Alana Newfield is on page one:

MISSING KAUA'I WOMAN BEARS SIGNATURE OF STRANGLER

"The body of Alana Newfield, found naked above Waimea Canyon late Friday afternoon, bore a crude line drawing of a wave cigarette-burned on her chest. The daughter of County Prosecutor-elect Janson Newfield had been missing since Halloween evening on the Garden Isle. Frightened residents of the normally peaceful island are absorbing the shock that the Barking Sands Strangler appears to be back."

Alana's death does in fact mirror the deaths of Jennifer Reece, Elise Morneau, and Tara Marie Havens. And her body was found in the same locale where the Strangler disposed of theirs.

I turn on the TV to a local morning talk show. The topic is the apparent return of the Strangler. Already fear has overtaken the Garden Isle, given the daunting prospect that Alana Newfield's murder signals his return.

My phone rings. It's Maile.

I brief her on the latest news from Kaua'i. She's sorry for the family of Alana Newfield. She understands my need to return to Kaua'i and assures me that she'll relieve me soon.

"Where are you?" I ask.

"Palm Springs. Actually, Indian Wells—at one of those exclusive country clubs where multi-million-dollar homes grace lush golf links. The club is called The Sphinx. Members only."

"Are you taking up golf?"

"I wish. Brittanie's brought the dog here. I'm camped out by the grand entrance—a fan-palm festooned pyramid between incoming and outgoing lanes. I've already made fast friends with the security detail."

"Why did Brittanie take the dog there?"

"Her grandfather lives here. Turns out he just lost his wife and he's not doing well. But if Brittanie thinks Precious would be safer from Boz here, she's in for a surprise. She doesn't know about me yet."

"She must be super angry if she goes to that extreme."

"She may have other reasons for stealing Boz's dog than he's telling us. I bet there's more to the story."

"You going to wrap this up soon? Tomorrow's Monday and I've got to get back to Kaua'i."

"Great," she says. "You can return Precious."

"You'll have her here by tomorrow?"

"Tonight, if I'm lucky," Maile says. "Hold on Kai . . . good news. Brittanie and the old man and Precious are heading for the gate in a big Lincoln. Gotta go. Here they come. Wish me luck."

"You got it."

An hour later Maile texts: "Have Precious. Heading for LAX."

Monday morning Maile calls from her Mānoa cottage. She sounds half asleep but offers to pay my flight to Līhu'e if I deliver Precious to Boz today. Since I need to talk to Boz anyway and I like the free plane ride I accept. I don't know what I'm getting into delivering the pooch, but Maile makes it sound simple and straightforward. Soon she's on her way to Lanikai with the Skye terrier.

Monday's paper carries more news about Alana Newfield. Her clothes have turned up in the West Side town of Kekaha in a convenience store dumpster. Spiked high heels. Sequined dress.

Was she decked out for a Halloween party when she went missing? Or was she in her professional attire? Her clothes could contain a treasure trove of DNA evidence. No doubt Kaua'i Police are on it.

Maile shows up at the Van Ormes' with the cute little terrier in tow—silver platinum coat, bangs nearly covering her eyes. Kula, who towers over Precious, is anxious to meet her. The terrier shies away. He sniffs her until she gives him a little growl. Kula, always the gentleman, backs off. Before I take Precious to the airport Maile tells me how she recovered the Skye terrier, since Boz may ask me to explain.

Maile followed Brittanie and her grandfather to a trendy Palm Springs restaurant where well-heeled patrons bring their pampered pooches. The two took a booth on an alfresco veranda beneath kerosene heaters blazing against a morning chill.

"I waited while they ordered," the pet detective explains, "figuring my only chance would be if Brittanie got up from the table. She seemed attentive to her grandfather. The more I followed her, the more I doubted Boz's story about her."

"She's no typical pet thief?"

"Not at all. Anyway, through the entire meal Brittanie and her grandfather hovered over their plates."

"So how did you pull it off?"

"The old man eventually needed to use the restroom. Brittanie started to help him but then remembered Precious. I saw and offered to watch the dog.

"Brilliant!"

"When Brittanie escorted her grandfather out of sight, I carried Precious to my rental car and headed for the LA airport."

Maile's cell phone rings.

It's her client. Boz's wife is on her way from Rome via San Francisco to Honolulu, and he's freaked. When she lands she's catching a Hawaiian Airlines flight to Līhuʻe. Precious must to be home before then, he insists. Maile reassures him that she's sending a fellow agent with the dog today.

"You've got to beat her here!" I can hear him scream.

"We'll do our best," Maile replies.

When she hangs up, Maile gets on her phone and checks Hawaiian Airlines flights from Honolulu to Līhuʻe. It's now nearly 10:00 am and the next flight leaves at 10:35. Can't make that one. The following flight goes at 12:05 pm. She books me on that one, paying my fare as she promised. Precious will be my carry-on, Maile says. No seat. No charge.

"Mahalo," I say. "I'll give it my best shot."

She texts me Boz's address in Princeville, then coaxes the Skye terrier into her small carrier and I rush to the airport. I check in, get through security, and head to the waiting area, hoping to beat Mrs. Elizabeth Boz to Līhu'e.

Precious is calm. She seems not sure of me yet, but she makes hardly a peep in her carrier.

At the gate, twenty minutes before departure, passengers have already gathered. We're sitting quietly as a few more passengers file in. Suddenly Precious starts to bark. An ample, pleasant-looking woman in a dark blazer glances in our direction.

Could that be her?

seventeen

I rush Precious out of the waiting area. She stops barking. If that's Mrs. Boz and she's on the same airplane with us, how am I going to keep her from seeing Precious? And even if I'm so lucky as to keep the Skye Terrier out of her sight, how am I going to get Precious home before she arrives?

I call Maile. She says she'll call her client.

Maile gets back to me right way. "Kai, Elizabeth Boz is on the same flight as you."

"*Auwe!*"

"Her husband is driving from Princeville to Līhuʻe as we speak to pick her up. And now he's even more freaked."

"Tell Boz to stall his return home with his wife so I can get to Princeville first. He can figure out some excuse why I'm with Precious. Tell her I'm a dog groomer, or whatevah."

"I'll call him back now." With that, Maile is gone.

Since Boz owns his own business and lives in ritzy Princeville, I assume he's well-to-do and I hope that means his wife flies first class. If I'm lucky, she'll board with elite passengers before me and everyone else in the economy cabin. I will have to parade Precious by her to get to my seat.

Fortunately, the ventilated sides of the carrier have fold-down covers so Precious can't see out and her mistress can't see in. If Mrs. Boz is not in first class and instead riding in back with me, the game may be up.

When it's time to board, sure enough, Elizabeth Boz walks down the jetway with first-class passengers. Five minutes later I file by her carrying Precious, blocking Mrs. Boz's view of the pet carrier with my personal carryon. As long as the Skye terrier doesn't squeal we should skate by. Elizabeth Boz's has smartly trimmed dark hair and her blazer looks crisp, considering all the miles she's flown. I whiff the pleasant scent she's wearing as I pass by. She exudes a good vibe. Does she deserve better than what I've heard so far of her husband? Or is she more like him than she appears?

I find my seat in the back of the airplane and hold Precious on my lap. My cell phone chimes. A text from Maile.

"Kai, Boz says he'll take his time getting back to Princeville. His wife has to wait for her luggage, anyway, and then he'll stop to buy some champagne for their happy reunion."

"Happy reunion?" I text back. "Tell him to stall. I've got to rent a car and then chug up to Princeville."

"Drive like the wind," Maile says.

"On tourist-clogged Kūhiō Highway? It'll be a close shave and the guy we're doing it for sounds like he hardly deserves it."

"Agree," Maile replies. "But at least you get a contact for your case."

Before I can reply the airplane pushes back and soon taxis and takes off. Then a brief climb and an equally brief descent. When the jet pulls to the gate at Līhu'e Airport, first-class passengers disembark before the rest of us. Elizabeth Boz has a five-minute head start. But she has to wait for her luggage, which can be slow process at neighbor island airports.

I tote Precious through the terminal, carrier flaps still down. In baggage claim I see Mrs. Boz. She's with the man I assume is her husband and Maile's client. He's holding his wife's hand, but they're standing far apart, not close like reunited lovers. He looks vaguely familiar. He's youthful, mid- forties, abundant brown hair, fashionable stubble. I can picture him attracting a naïve young woman. But does he resemble the police sketch of the Strangler twenty years later?

Boz spots me with the dog carrier. He doesn't know me, but he knows the carrier. He tenses, then nods. I nod back.

I catch a bus to the car rental agencies, pick up my vehicle, and soon Precious and I are cruising up Kūhiō Highway along the ocean toward Princeville. The traffic is light for this time of day. Not as bad as I expected.

Just shy of Hanalei, I turn in at Princeville's swanky seaside golf resorts and upscale condos and homes. From the address Maile has given me, Boz must live in one of the ocean view homes.

Sure enough, it's a rambling place in a cul-de-sac over-looking lovely Hanalei Bay. I park down the block and wait as I've been instructed. A dark blue Mercedes pulls into the driveway. Once Boz pops the trunk I pull up with Precious. He steps toward me. He's got riveting blue eyes and comely regular features. Close enough to the police sketch.

Boz has been instructed by Maile what to say. He introduces me to his wife in smooth tones as a dog groomer. She hardly notices me she's so overjoyed to see Precious. And the terrier to see her owner. I hand the pet carrier to Mrs. Boz, as pleasant up close as she appeared from a distance on the airplane. When she and the terrier are out of earshot I mention to Boz that I dropped by his kayak rental business in Hanalei a few days ago. I don't say why. Boz seems puzzled.

"I'll be going now," I say, convinced this is not the time to interview him.

He pulls out his wallet and hands me a hundred-dollar bill.

"That's not necessary, sir."

"Sure it is," he replies. "I can't thank you enough."

"Very generous. Thank you, sir."

I notice a cut on his right forearm—well, two cuts, parallel red lines about an inch apart and several inches long. Two band-aids partially cover the wounds. Looks like he's been scratched by a pair of fingernails. Alana Newfield's fingernails?

"Nasty cuts," I say.

"Gardening accident," he explains hastily. "I've got two green thumbs, but neither is very coordinated. I've blown through a whole box of band-aids!"

If this wound actually comes from a struggle with Alana— one last desperate grasp while fighting for her life—DNA from the wounds might confirm. But how to snag one of Boz's band-aids, aside from ripping it off his arm?

I hold that thought as we continue to chat. Before long Boz gestures behind him toward the ocean view home to which both his wife and her Precious have just returned.

"I better be going." He winks.

He heads for his front door and I for my rental car. He's inside the house when I notice a gray rubbish container at the end of his driveway that says PROPERTY OF COUNTY OF KAUA'I. It's the kind with hinged lid and wheels designed for automated pickup. Since dumpster diving is one of my favorite activities I flip open the lid.

Inside are three bulging plastic kitchen bags. I don't want to be seen sorting through Boz's rubbish. So I make a snap decision. I grab the two bags on top, pop the trunk of my rental car, and toss them in.

Leaving Princeville, I head toward Līhu'e on Kūhiō Highway. I pull off in less than a mile and park along the roadside. I pop the trunk and open one of the trash bags. It doesn't take long. Boz wasn't kidding about blowing through a box of band-aids. I find a half dozen bloody samples.

If Boz is the guy these bloody band-aids could prove it. I leave them in the bags. And leave the bags in the trunk. I motor toward Kaua'i Police headquarters with my prize.

eighteen

A few miles down the road I pull off again and call Maile.

"Remember I told you I wanted to talk to Ian Boz?"

"Yeah," she says.

"Well, I got a blood sample from him."

"He agreed?"

"I went through his garbage. Standard procedure."

"Boz may be a cheater, but a murderer? I never featured him for that. He told me he tossed Brittanie's belongings onto his front lawn to force her out. And that's why she took revenge by stealing his wife's dog."

"Assuming Boz's story was true. Did you see her things on his lawn?"

"I saw none of it. And I told you already, Kai, I had my doubts. My case was to recover the dog. And I did. Clients don't always tell me the truth. My main concern is if they can prove they own the dog they want me to recover. And Boz could."

"Did you talk to Brittanie?"

"Not much. The only words I exchanged with her came when she left me in charge of the dog."

"Nothing after that?"

"Nope. I think Brittanie knew she couldn't prove Precious was hers."

"I want to talk to Brittanie about Ian Boz."

"You'll find her either in Palm Springs or Burbank," the pet detective replies.

"Did Boz give you her number?"

"Nope."

"Would you call him and get it for me?" I did Maile a favor and figure she'll do one for me.

"What do I say is the reason? If he's got something to hide, like cheating on his wife, is he going to cough up Brittanie's number?"

"It's worth a try."

"This is a no go, Kai." She's adamant. "He has just reunited with his wife. She may be suspicious about the dog delivery. He sounds like the kind of guy who arouses plenty of suspicion. He doesn't want to talk to me now—guaranteed."

"Where do Brittanie's parents live in Burbank?"

"Well, okay," she says. "Now we're getting somewhere. The street name is Poplar Avenue and the address—" I wait while she scrolls through her phone—"is 1527."

"And their name?"

"On the mailbox it said Langstrom."

"So, Brittanie Langstrom at 1527 Poplar Avenue in Burbank, California?"

"That's the best I can do. You can get a phone number for the house—but probably not Brittanie's cell number. You'll have to wangle that out of her parents."

"Okay. Thanks."

By now it's late afternoon on Kaua'i. And evening in California. I wish I had my laptop. I do a search on my cellphone without much success. Reception isn't great.

I drive down the highway to Kapa'a Public Library. Computers and free wi-fi. School is out for the afternoon and kids are cozying up to the screens and playing video games. Not one free computer. I go to the reference desk, show my Surfing Detective card, and explain I need to do one quick search. The reference librarian lets me use a computer behind the desk. I plug in Brittanie's name and address and am prompted that a phone number is available. But I have to pay. I try another site, and it actually gives me a number, area code 818. I write it down. I check a few more sites, white pages, etc. They all want money. Another free site pops up the same number.

I go with that.

I thank the librarian and return to my rental car. I call the number and a man answers.

"Mr. Langstrom?"

"Yes. Who's calling?" He sounds wary.

"I'm from Kaua'i small animal hospital and I'm following up about a Skye terrier we saw recently named Precious. May I speak to Brittanie?"

"I'm sorry she's not here."

"Do you have a number where I can reach her?"

"Well, it's a coincidence you called because Brittanie said the terrier was stolen in Palm Springs."

"Oh, no!" I try to sound alarmed.

"Yes, afraid so." Mr. Langstrom sighs.

"Well, maybe we can help with Precious's microchip

number."

"You better call her cell phone."

"Perfect," I say.

He gives me Brittanie's number. I thank him and immediately call.

"Brittanie," I say when she answers, "my name is Kai Cooke. I'm a private detective in Honolulu."

"How'd you get my number?" She too sounds wary.

"Your father gave it to me."

"Oh?" Her voice drops. "What's this about?"

"I'm investigating several murders on Kaua'i. All young women. All their cases are unsolved. Since I understand you were just on the island, I wondered if you might talk with me briefly—just answer a few questions that might help the investigation along."

"What's that got to do with me?"

"I want to talk with you about Ian Boz."

"Oh, *him,*" she says disgustedly.

"What can you tell me about Mr. Boz?"

Brittanie hesitates. "Well, I was foolish. I can see that now."

"How were you foolish?"

"I believed him when he offered free rent for watching his wife's dog while she was away."

"What was not to believe?" I ask the obvious, because it needs asking.

"He expected, I guess—" she hesitates. "Well, you know."

"I get it," I say. "And that wasn't your expectation?"

"No. I liked him at first. He was nice and soft-spoken. He was pleasant on the surface. And I thought since he was married and since he seemed like a nice man he would be okay. But right away he made me nervous."

"How did he make you nervous?"

"Once he wandered into the bathroom while I was taking a shower. When I saw him I screamed. He was very apologetic."

"Anything else like that happen?"

"Too often. He snuck into my bedroom one night when I was sleeping. And he barged in once when I was dressing."

"Then what?"

"I started looking for another place to live. It's hard to find a rental on short notice, except in a hotel, which I couldn't afford."

"Did he ever get physical with you? " I ask, wondering if those two red stripes on Boz's arm could have come from Brittanie rather than Alana Newfield.

"When he tried to touch me I pushed him away."

"Did you scratch his arm? Did you make him bleed?"

"I pushed him as hard as I could. Whether he bled or not, I don't know."

"Was that on Halloween?"

"Yes, Halloween was the day I left. When he went to work I returned to collect my things."

"And Precious too?"

"Yes."

"Why did you take the dog?"

"Because I hated Boz and I didn't trust him to care for Precious. Soon he came looking for me—I was hiding out with friends—and eventually he hired someone to follow me. I didn't feel safe on the island even with friends so I decided to fly home to my parents in Burbank."

"With the dog?"

"I know it may have been wrong, but at the time I didn't care."

"How did you get Precious through security?"

"I had copies of her papers."

"What happened once you arrived in LA?"

"My parents already have a Maltese so they couldn't keep Precious. They suggested I take her to my grandfather who lives in Palm Springs. He's alone. My grandmother recently passed away."

"I'm sorry."

"Thanks. It's been really hard for him. Anyway, I drove down there and delivered Precious. But then a woman, probably sent by Ian, ran off with her."

"When you were dog-sitting for him did Boz ever talk about other dog-sitters or other women? Or did he have any mementos—photographs, jewelry, or articles of women's clothing that you might have stumbled upon?"

"Not that I can remember. But from chatting with another dog sitter I found out I wasn't his first victim. He has a reputation. I should have talked with Cassie before I took the job."

"Cassie? Can you text me Cassie's number?"

"Sure. And I can tell you about a few other creeps I've run into on this island. And still more other sitters have told me about."

"I'd like that. I'll check back with you."

"Anything I can do to stop that man."

nineteen

I drive to Kaua'i Police Headquarters in Līhu'e, pull the two trash bags from the trunk, and climb the stairs to Nakamura's office. Getting them through security takes some coaxing. Nakamura looks at the two bags and then at me. "We're not a public landfill, you know?"

I pluck a few of the bloodied band-aids and display them. "These could lead to your Strangler."

"Who do they belong to?"

"Ian Boz. He runs a kayak rental business in Hanalei. He resembles your police sketch from twenty years ago. These band-aids covered a wound that probably came from a struggle with someone. Possibly Alana Newfield."

"How did you get the sample?"

"From the suspect's trash dumpster. Mail in the bags identifies him. He lives in Princeville. I just delivered his wife's stolen dog, recovered by my pet detective colleague."

"Pet detective?" Nakamura raises her brows. "Did you get his permission for the samples?"

"Just run them and if you get a match you can request a warrant for an official sample," I say. "Fernandez told me HPD has a Rapid DNA Machine that can produce results in ninety minutes."

"Our department doesn't have that machine, Kai. Even if we did I doubt I could run these bloody band-aids, considering."

"Suit yourself." I shove the band-aids into one of the trash bags and start to haul both bags away.

"Wait," she says. I turn back. "You've got a good relationship with Frank Fernandez, right?"

"I wouldn't say good. But we do talk."

"Get Frank to run the samples on HPD's machine and send the results over to us. If it's a match with the DNA extracted from Alana's clothes then we pursue Boz."

"I've used up all my favors with Fernandez. Why would he do this for me?"

"Tell him he'll share the credit for catching the Barking Sands Strangler."

"You promise? I don't want to feed Frank a line."

"Use my name, Kai. Tell him I said it's a go. He helps us on this case he shares the credit for closing it."

"I'll be on my way then."

"Hold on," she says. "I'll get you proper evidence bags." She's gone for a while and then returns wearing gloves and holding two clear plastic bags. She picks up the two band-aids with tweezers and slips one into each bag.

"I'll leave the other samples with you." I gesture to the bulging white trash bags, doubting I can take them on an airplane. "And other identifying evidence the bags contain."

"Mahalo, Kai," she says deadpan. "I'll keep them until we hear from Fernandez."

As I close the door behind me I feel like I've won the battle, if not the war. But if this DNA sample leads nowhere my credibility with Frank and with Nakamura erodes further. Much more erosion and I'll have no ground to stand on.

I head across the highway to Līhu'e Airport. There's no way to get these bloody band-aids to Fernandez quickly except to hand-carry them myself. I suddenly second-guess my gut feeling about Boz. What if I'm wrong? I still believe Boz is connected, somehow. I'll keep going with that for now.

At Līhu'e Airport I'm a day early with both the rental car and my return flight. Turning in the car early is a breeze. I get a small refund. Flying home a day early is not. Used to be a passenger could stand by for any interisland flight. Didn't matter what day or time. You waited until all ticketed passengers boarded and then any empty seats were fair game.

It's more complicated these days. You can standby on the same day for an earlier or later flight to your destination if your fare class is still available. If not, you pay the difference between fares. And a change fee. I'm lucky. It's early afternoon, flights are not crowded, and my fare class is available. I pay only the change fee, get my ticket switched, slog through security, and head to the gate.

Before long a jet from Honolulu pulls to the gate, passengers unload, and those of us returning to O'ahu file onto the airplane. In my carry-on, in two plastic evidence bags, ride the band-aids that I'm hoping will crack the Barking Sands case.

Once back in Honolulu I drive to Honolulu Police headquarters on Beretania Street. It's now close to 4:00 pm. And a roll of the dice whether Frank Fernandez will be in.

There's good news. And bad news.

Fernandez is in. But I'm told he's in a foul mood.

I'm ushered into Frank's office. He is, in fact, looking glum. He glances up from his desk, sees me, and looks down again.

"What's wrong, Frank?"

"It's Blitz," he says.

"Your Rottweiler?"

"He's gone."

"Gone where?"

"I don't know. Maile's housesitting in Lanikai and Blitz was alone in her cottage while I'm at work. I got a call from one of her neighbors that he was wandering the streets of Mānoa."

I shake my head. That doesn't sound good. "You're married to the best pet detective in the islands," I try to encourage him. "Maile will find him."

"She can't leave. Whoever owns that Lanikai mansion is on their way home and Maile has to hand off the place to them."

"The Van Ormes," I say. "I thought they were staying away until Tuesday?"

"Their plans apparently changed."

"I'm sure as soon as they return Maile will find Blitz."

"Damn." Fernandez' eyes moisten.

Frank looks genuinely stricken. I've never seen him show such tender emotions. I have a quick think.

"Look, Frank. I worked with Maile before. I know some of her tricks of the trade. I'll drive up to Mānoa and have look for Blitz."

He brightens. "You'd do that, Kai?"

"I would."

Then he looks suspicious. "What brings you here, anyway?"

"I've got a small favor. Won't take long. Little or no effort on your part."

"What favor?"

I pull out the evidence bag with the two bloody band-aids. "In this bag is a potential DNA sample that may nail a cold case twenty years old. Two samples of the same blood. The blood, maybe, of the Barking Sands Strangler."

"What's that got to do with me?"

"Okay, Frank, here's the deal. Nakamura wants this DNA sample, but she doesn't have a Rapid DNA Machine that HPD has. She promises if you get your lab to run this sample she'll share the credit with you. You just run the sample and send the results to her, the sooner the better."

"How do you know this is the guy?"

"I don't know."

Fernandez groans.

"Tell you what, Frank, you get this into your DNA machine and I'll be off to Mānoa." I give him Nakamura's contact information and hand him the evidence bags.

"I'm going to search for Blitz. I'll call when I have good news. What do you say, Frank?"

I leave him looking dubious.

I head up into the Mānoa Valley and stop by Maile's cottage. She's not there, of course. I call her. She reminds me how to proceed. There's no time to post signs, she says. That can be done later, if necessary. She tells me to start at her cottage and search outward, making wider and wider circles. She says to hold that pattern and canvass the entire valley. She promises to meet me later with Kula when the Van Ormes return.

I chart wide circles starting from Maile's cottage. Near the top of the valley I come upon the Mānoa Chinese cemetery where one night Kula had a close scrape with death. Dog thief Spyder Silva pulled his Berretta on Maile and me and fired. Kula who'd already been freed from the canine crook jumped on Silva. My boy's yelp when Silva's Berretta went off again was the most frightening sound I've ever heard. Kula lay motionless. The only reason I can recall it now is because the golden came home from the veterinary hospital good as new. But between that gunshot and Kula's release was a long, dark road I never want to walk again. Silva did not make it home from the cemetery that night. For that I take full responsibility. Since Silva's handgun had been drawn and twice fired, Fernandez and his fellow officers in Homicide understood why I pulled my Smith & Wesson. Self-defense.

Speaking of Frank, I scan grave markers on this night years later and don't see his Rottweiler. I keep searching. I stop and ask passersby. Nobody has seen Blitz. Time goes by and I hear nothing from Maile. Or from Frank. Did he run the bloody band-aids? I'd like to deliver his Rottie just as Fernandez delivers the DNA evidence.

Things seldom work out so smoothly.

twenty

Later that night I meet up with Maile at her cottage and she delivers Kula. He hops in my car, wagging and crooning. I tell Maile the streets I've searched for Blitz, mostly in the upper valley, wish her luck, and then head over the Pali Highway to Kailua.

Tuesday morning I awake to a text from Maile, sent a little after 1:00 am. She found Blitz wandering in lower Mānoa. He was dusty and dehydrated and needed a bath, but otherwise okay. She thanks me for my search in the upper valley, which helped her focus her search on the lower.

"Frank must be relieved," I text back.

"I don't know," she replies instantly. "He didn't come home last night."

"He's still at the station?"

"Your guess is as good as mine."

"When you talked to him earlier did he mention a DNA sample?"

"We talked only about Blitz. What's this about?"

"My Kaua'i case."

"Don't know, Kai. Why don't you call him?"

I phone Fernandez's office and get his voicemail. I leave a message. I call his cell phone and do the same. Not hearing from him is starting to bother me.

Before heading to my office I receive an email from Acme Insurance, the mainland company that hired me for that fraud investigation. They like the photos I took earlier of the kite surfer at Ke'ehi Lagoon. But now they want videos showing him in motion.

I call a surfing buddy who's a concierge at the Waikīkī hotel where the kite surfer, Reginald Bowman, is staying. I learn Bowman plans to go kiting this morning at Kailua Beach Park, a few blocks from Vivienne's home. It's a no brainer. Instead of waiting around for Fernandez to call I hop in my car and head to the beach park.

It's breezy—a typical trade-wind pattern kicking up surf and bending palms around the white-sand crescent of Kailua Bay. I step from my car to the sound of fronds clacking in the breeze. These are the kind of conditions that bring out wind- and kite-surfers in droves. I'm at the north end of the park at the designated launch area where I expect to find Bowman. Sure enough, within minutes a rental car pulls up with my subject and his girlfriend aboard.

Bowman hops out and so does his companion. She sheds her beach coverup to reveal youthful curves that must keep Reggie's middle-aged heart pumping. She's got surfer muscles too. Might that be her attraction to him—a free surfing safari to Hawai'i?

Reginald Bowman is a water-sports enthusiast who was involved in a minor fender-bender, which he claims resulted in neck and back pain that have impeded his ability to support his family. His lawyer has sued, even though X-rays showed no broken bones or other irregularities. Despite Bowman's injury claims he has slipped away with his girlfriend for a long weekend in Hawai'i. His wife and three kids didn't make the trip. I have been following him. I already tracked him to Ke'ehi Lagoon, as I mentioned, and snapped photos of him kite surfing there.

Now Acme wants videos. So, I'll give Acme videos.

Bowman lugs his gear to in the kite surf rigging area, a long grassy lawn just inland of graceful ironwoods lining the beach. I step from my car, slip behind a green *naupaka*-covered dune, and start videoing him with my phone. He unceremoniously drops his kite bag, pump, and board on the grass in a gesture that says *I don't give a rip*. His girlfriend doesn't even blink. But other kiters nearby give him a look— knowing how expensive kite gear can be. She may be used to his attitude, but they are not. I see them making mental notes to be wary of this guy in the water.

Soon Bowman is stretching out the lines attached to his kite and making sure they're not crossed or tangled. He clicks his control bar into his waist harness, grabs his board under a free arm, and signals his girlfriend with a thumbs-up. She picks up his kite with a flick of one foot and leads him down to the beach.

I emerge from the dune and follow them at a distance as she valets his gear to the water. These two are a well-oiled machine. I continue to record as I follow them, then I step behind an ironwood for cover. I video Bowman as he gets set, giving his girlfriend another thumbs up, and she releases the kite into the air.

"Smooth, brah." I say under my breath. And capture it all.

Bowman then lifts his kite into enough wind to drag him through the shore break away from swimmers in the shallow water, leans back, puts his feet into the board's foot straps, and launches himself.

Bowman doesn't waste any time giving me exactly what I came for. Not even ten seconds from his takeoff point, he leaps into a jump that has kiters on the beach turning their heads. I tilt my phone skyward to capture the rising arc of his board. At the highest point he unhooks his control bar from the safety harness and twirls around twice before reattaching and landing smoothly. Kiters call this a Deuce 360. And you don't often see it. Maybe on Maui, where the winds blow stronger and the kiters are more expert. But here in sleepy Kailua?

Bowman may be a skilled kite surfer—not to mention a show off—but he hasn't got neck and back pain. *No way.*

"Got ya!" I whisper to myself.

Soon I have more than enough video to satisfy Acme Insurance. Good news. I could use a check from Acme while waiting on the Ossendorfer case.

By afternoon I'm back on Maunakea Street and I still haven't heard from Fernandez. My office phone eventually rings. Caller ID says not HPD but Kaua'i Police Department.

"Kai," says Detective Nakamura. "It's a match."

"What's a match?"

"Your buddy Fernandez emailed me the DNA results last night. Boz is a match."

"Ian Boz is the Barking Sands Strangler?"

"We've only just brought him in. And he's willing to give

another sample. We don't need a court order."

"He's willing?"

"Yes. What we do know with relative certainty, pending DNA evidence from the new sample, is that semen found on Alana's dress the night she was abducted and killed came from Boz."

"Hmmm."

"Gotta go," Nakamura says. "After we interview him I'll be in touch."

My head is spinning. It's hard to argue with DNA evidence. But as much as I banked on this, I realize now that I didn't really expect it.

The rest of the day I can't concentrate. But I do have the presence of mind to make a few calls. I leave a message for Fernandez, thanking him for running the DNA test and sending the results to Nakamura.

Then I call my client. I tell Mrs. Reece that we may have a major break in the Alana Newfield case. And that break could lead to a break in Jennifer's case. I explain that I can't say much more, just that it involves a suspect who resembles a police sketch and has been positively linked to the victim. Mrs. Reece is elated.

The day goes by and I hear nothing more from Nakamura.

Tuesday evening I meet Vivienne's return flight from San Francisco. Her beaming smile feels like a flood of sunshine. Suddenly we're both talking a mile a minute, trying to catch up for days and nights apart. She enjoyed her conference in Berkeley and she's getting more and more excited about the baby. Her excitement is infectious. I tell her I'm cautiously optimistic about the DNA match in the Barking Sands case. And I wonder out loud if the Boz match will mean the end to the investigation. When we arrive home Viv is bushed from her conference and still on California time. She crashes early. I'm not sleepy yet but I climb into bed next to her and listen to the rise and fall of her breathing. A peaceful hour goes by like this. Then I join her in dreamland.

Wednesday morning I walk Kula on Kailua Beach. Then Viv and I breakfast together, chat more about our time apart, and pour over the local newspaper. In the neighbor island section there's no news from the Garden Isle. The Kaua'i Police Department is apparently withholding information about the DNA match in the Alana Newfield case. No doubt they will wait until they complete their investigation of Ian Boz.

Later that morning in my office Frank Fernandez calls.

"Boz not the guy." Frank says matter-of-factly. "I just heard from KPD."

"Boz is a DNA match, right?"

"He's a match. But he's not the guy. That was his semen on Alana Newfield's dress, all right. But he didn't abduct her and he didn't kill her. And there's no evidence he was involved in the earlier murders."

"Boz has an ironclad alibi?"

"He was the Newfield girl's customer on Halloween night before she was abducted. Did you know she was a working girl?"

"I did."

"Well, Boz apparently hooked up with her in a Princeville hotel room. I guess he was careless, Kai, because he made a mess of her dress. Yet he claims he didn't have sex with her."

"How does he explain the semen?"

"Doesn't matter. Whatever they did in that room he's not the guy."

"What makes KPD so sure?"

"After he was with Alana, Boz went to the hotel bar. The hotel's security cameras confirm. He sat there drinking for another hour. Before he departed security footage shows Alana Newfield leaving the hotel. Alone. Not with Boz."

"What about after that?"

"Get this, Kai, Boz hooked up with another working girl."

"Another?"

"Yes, two on the same night in the same hotel but in different rooms. He's not saying what he did with the second woman or who she was."

"Figures."

"But there's no doubt he was still in the hotel because cameras show him walking the halls. He didn't leave the hotel until midnight on Halloween, a couple hours after Alana left. The timing isn't right. He couldn't have done it."

I shake my head. "I had it figured Boz got riled when his live-in dogwalker and intended plaything took off with his absent wife's terrier earlier on Halloween day. And his anger spilled over."

"You had it figured wrong, Kai." Frank says, "Boz looked like the police sketch of the Strangler and looked like Alana's killer, but he's neither. And that DNA favor I did you came to nothing."

"Can't win 'em all," I reply. "I owe you Frank. And I better call my client and break the bad news."

"Good luck with that." Fernandez hangs up.

twenty-one

Boz is not the guy. Fernandez's words ring in my ears. My strongest lead has led to a curious dead end. And I'm not sure where to go from here.

I head to Rockpiles.

Rockpiles is a town surf spot offshore of the Ala Wai Yacht Harbor. The name comes from the harbor's lava rock jetty and channel. I pull up to the small boat harbor and park by Waikīkī's legendary Ilikai Hotel, where Jack Lord posed for the opening of the original *Hawaii Five-O* TV series. You might remember the drum roll, the twanging guitars, and the cascading wave that started the show, while from high up Lord's character, Detective Steve McGarrett, turned steely eyes to the camera. That kind of glamour has never been my lot as a private detective. But I'll skip the glamour any day for a good wave.

I strip down to my board shorts and beach flips and tote my board to the harbor jetty. Rockpiles can be an especially good break in summer. With traffic to match. But in November, like elsewhere on the south shore, waves are smaller and so are the crowds. The hollow peaks and occasional tubes of the warm season give way to gentle rollers that crest over a shallow coral reef. Even in small surf, boards that wash against the lava rock jetty—and the surfers who ride them—can end up badly dinged. Surfing has its hazards. Like detective work. Such as spending your client's money and coming up with next to nothing. I warned Mrs. Reece this might happen. She urged me on anyway.

That's why I've come to Rockpiles. To figure out what's next.

I scale the seawall, put my board in the water, say my mantra, and paddle out. Small surf has its advantages. I have the place to myself. The little rollers are topping out just above my knees. But it's nice. Calm and quiet except for the occasional boat chugging out the harbor channel.

Before long I spot a set rolling in, swing my board around, and catch the first wave. It breaks left, so I go left too, my back side to the face. I'm a regular-foot surfer. I plant a rail and stay well ahead of the curling lip. Trimming to a smooth plane, I cross-step forward and hang my pinkies over my board's tip. *Toes on the nose!* I'm a hot-dogger on these bantam waves, especially with no one watching.

After this nose ride I paddle back into the lineup and park myself on my well-waxed deck. As I straddle my board and wait for another little beauty, the soothing sea puts me in the mood for thought.

I need to get moving again on my search for the Barking Sands Strangler. Talking once more to Ian Boz might actually be a good start. He may have been the last person to see Alana Newfield alive, other than her abductor—the Strangler himself? I know Boz will have been grilled by KPD, but I don't expect Nakamura to say much about that. I do wonder what Boz told his wife about why Kaua'i Police questioned him. I'm sure he came up with something. He's obviously clever. Whatever he told law enforcement, I'll have to hear it from him personally.

A few more ripping-good rides put me in another mood—the mood to be with Vivienne. I scale that seawall again, carry my board back to my car, towel off, and head over the Pali to Kailua. Viv isn't home yet so I walk Kula on the beach. When we return she's lying in bed, exhausted from her first day back in the classroom after her conference in Berkeley. I ask if there's anything I can do.

"I'm too beat to make dinner," she says. "But I'd love a cheese omelet."

"I'll bring it to you," I say. "How about some buttered toast?"

She nods. "That would be lovely. I didn't get much sleep last night."

Before long I'm cracking eggs and shredding cheese. Butter is soon melting in a frypan. Two slices of bread poised in the toaster. I'm actually pretty fair at making omelets. Timing is everything—when to add the cheese and when to fold and flip. Too early—it's runny. Too late—it's crispy. You want the omelet right there in that succulent middle.

When omelet and toast are ready I walk them to Vivienne. She's asleep. I set the plate on her nightstand and tiptoe from the room. I feed Kula, make another omelet for myself, and watch the local evening news.

Kaua'i Police have announced they are making progress on Alana Newfield's murder, but of course don't give specifics. I wonder what breakthroughs they could be referring to, other than the DNA evidence I provided connecting Ian Boz to the victim. Unless Nakamura has something she not sharing.

The next morning the case is pulling me back to Kauaʻi. Viv's feeling better. I ask if she's well enough to manage without me for a day or two and welcome her reassurance.

I book a late-morning flight to Līhuʻe. By noon I'm driving north on Kūhiō Highway toward Hanalei. I stop in at Ian Boz's kayak shop. The same surfer is working the rental counter.

"I remember you," he says. "You brought in that sketch that looked like my boss."

"Is he here today?" I ask.

"He is. So is his wife."

"His wife?"

"And her dog Precious. They're in his office." He gestures behind him, as the raised voice of a woman resounds from behind the door. She doesn't sound happy.

"Would you please ask if I can see him?" I hand the clerk my card.

"Surfing Detective?" He looks at the board rider and raises his brow.

I nod as the voices—now his along with hers—behind the door grow louder.

The clerk knocks on the office door. It opens to a red-faced Boz who's not happy his tangle with his wife has been interrupted. The clerk shows him my card. Boz looks up at me and says to his clerk, "Tell the dog groomer to come back later."

The clerk returns with confused look. "Dog groomer?"

I say, "I'll just wait."

The clerk shakes his head.

I wander around the shop looking at kayaks and stand-up paddle boards and snorkel gear that Boz rents for having fun in the water. I keep an eye on his office door and an ear to the voices seeping through. Before long Elizabeth Boz pops out with a blush in her face and Precious in her arms. Her husband is close behind. She strides stiffly toward the door, glancing at me as she passes by. She recognizes me. So does the Skye terrier.

"What's your dog groomer doing here?" she asks her husband.

I pet Precious while the flustered Boz figures out what to say.

"Honey, I promised him some referrals."

She looks skeptical and asks me, "Are you in on this conspiracy?"

I shrug. I've learned the hard way: say the truth or say nothing.

She shakes her head and walks out the door. I glance back over the counter where the clerk has heard every word. He's looking even more confused.

I've become a mystery.

twenty-two

"You again?" Boz grunts. "What do you want?"

"A chat."

"C'mon and let's get this over with." He turns around and steps back into his office. I follow.

He sits behind his desk and I sit across from his riveting blue eyes. His stubble is gone. He's looking more clean-cut today.

I hand him my card, wondering if he knows I threw him under the bus. Did he see me going through his garbage? Did Nakamura tell him how she got his DNA sample?

"I had nothing to do with that girl's murder," he announces. "I'm not the Barking Sands Strangler."

"I know."

"And do you also know what kind of trouble this has brought into my house?"

"Any trouble in your house is of your own making."

"My wife is angry as hell. She's knows I've had contact with the girl who died. And she wants to know why."

"I could tell her," I say, recalling that she no doubt floats Boz's business. "But that's not why I'm here. I'm trying to solve three murders that happened twenty years ago. Maybe you can help. You were might be the last person to see Alana Newfield before she was abducted. Her murder appears to be related."

"I've been over that with the police. Repeatedly."

"But not with me."

"Have them fill you in."

"They won't. I need to hear it from you."

"Why should I bother?"

"I know about Brittanie," I say. "And I know about Alana. And I know about other women who've been in your house when your wife's away."

"Like who?"

"Cassie." I trot out the name of the dog-sitter Brit mentioned.

"If you believe anything Cassie tells you, you can't be much of a detective. Alana was a professional. Cassie is an amateur. But she likes cash as much as Alana."

"Look, I don't want to make more trouble for you. I just want a little help."

"You tell Brittanie and Cassie to steer clear of my wife and then maybe we'll talk."

"Tell me about Alana," I forge ahead. "Did she say or do anything that stood out to you that Halloween night at the resort?"

"Not really. We just kidded around. Light talk, you know. She was young."

"I know. But anything you can remember?"

"Well, on second thought, I must have said something that made her think of her father."

"Janson Newfield, the County Prosecutor-elect?"

"She didn't give his name. And I didn't find out until I heard on the news."

"What did she say about him?"

"I can't recall her exact words."

"Can you remember the gist?"

"Only that I got the impression she didn't like him."

"She's not alone," I press on. "What gave you that impression?"

Boz rises from his chair. "That's enough for now."

Back in my rental car I phone Brittanie.

"Regarding your dog-sitter friend, Cassie," I say, "can you tell me about her encounters with Boz?"

"Cassie got the same treatment from Boz I did," Brittanie says. "I should have talked to her before I took the job!"

"Boz tried to tell me that Cassie was an amateur hooker."

"That's a lie!" Brittanie replies. "Cassie is a really nice girl. With a steady boyfriend."

"Boz is bad, alright," I say. "But it turns out he's not the man I'm looking for."

"Weren't you going to make sure no other dog-sitter goes through what I did?"

"What you went through shouldn't happen again. Boz's wife is onto him now."

"Well, I hope so."

"I'm looking for another man—an even creepier man—who harasses and hurts women."

"Worse than Boz?"

"Definitely worse. Didn't you tell me about other dog-sitters—I mean besides Cassie—who've run into creepy guys?"

"Oh, you'd be surprised by the weirdos—like this guy on the West Side."

"West Side? Tell me about him."

"Another sitter said she found really strange stuff in the guy's house when he was away."

"Like what?"

"Like the things you asked me about before. Mementos."

"From women?"

"Girls, most likely. Photos. Necklaces. Blouses. Bras. He kept them around like souvenirs."

"What's his name?"

"Sorry, I'm drawing a blank."

"What's the sitter's name?"

"I've met her," Brit explains. "But I can't remember her name either."

"Take your time."

"It wasn't Cassie," she says. "It was another girl. I can see her face. I can even hear her voice. She's sweet. And gentle with dogs."

"Where does she live?"

"That I know. In Kilauea. Her parents own that popular bakery off Kūhiō Highway on the road to the lighthouse."

After the call I search on my phone for bakeries in Kilauea. Two hits. One is a chain pizza takeout. The other is called Kilauea Bake Shop. I punch in the numbers. The line is busy.

Lunchtime. No wonder.

Since I'm a stranger wishing to speak to the owners'

daughter, whose name I don't even know, I decide the only way to do this right is to go in person. I hop on Kūhiō Highway again. From Hanalei it's a journey of less than ten miles to Kilauea. I arrive to the buzzing lunch crowd. The café operates out of a repurposed yellow cottage with a covered *lānai*. I stand in line outside the cottage, then step in, order a sandwich, and ask about the owner's daughter, whose name turns out to be Silvie.

"I've heard Silvie is good dog-sitter."

An aproned man with longish graying hair steps up and replies. "I'm her father. Silvie's in Europe."

Auwe! I mumble to myself. "Where in Europe?"

"Last we heard, Amsterdam."

"Would you mind giving me her phone number?"

He looks me up and down. Makes a snap judgement. Then rattles off Silvie's number.

I take my sandwich and the phone number to a canopied outdoor table.

Amsterdam is twelve hours ahead of Hawai'i, says my phone's world clock. So lunchtime here is after midnight there. Should I wait and call her tomorrow? Nah, I'll text her now. She should get my message in the morning.

"Hi Silvie, I'm at your parents' bakery in Kilauea and have a few questions about your dog-sitting. Could we talk sometime soon?"

My cellphone almost immediately chimes. It's Silvie! "I'll return in about two weeks. When would you need me?"

"Thanks! For now, just a few questions. May I call you?"

"OK."

I enter her number and the twenty-something answers in

a voice surprisingly clear from half way around the world. I thank her again and say, "May I ask you about one of your dog-sitting experiences?"

"Sure."

"Another Kaua'i dog-sitter, Brittanie, told me you sat for a guy who lived on the West Side. She said you told her he had some creepy stuff in his house and that you would never work for him again. Do you remember him?"

"Why do you want to know?"

"To make sure what happened to you won't happen to anyone else. I'm a private detective."

There is a long pause. Have I lost her?

And then: "Good! That guy was spooky!"

"But you didn't report him to the police?"

"No. I didn't think he'd broken any laws. But I did warn other dog-sitters."

"What's the guy's name? Brit didn't remember."

"Moore."

"And his first name?"

"Uh, Michael—" She pauses. "No, Micah."

"Micah Moore?"

"That's him."

"Where does he live?"

"In Kekaha, on the West Side."

The location seems right. Kekaha is the West Side village a short drive from Barking Sands Beach where the first victim was found and at the foot of Waimea Canyon where remains of all three victims were discovered.

"Can you remember the street and number?"

"Not the number, but the street is called Hale Koa. And he

lives at the bend in the road."

"Mahalo! Brit said you told her Moore stored keepsakes of women—jewelry and clothing and underwear. Stuff like that. How did you find it? And where?"

"Ah, well, I wasn't exactly snooping around. I was looking for a dog leash. I checked in some of his rooms, you know?"

"That's okay. Just tell me what you found and where you found it."

"In his bedroom in the bottom dresser drawer. The kind of stuff you mentioned. Bras. Panties. Blouses. Some jewelry. They were girls or young women's things. They couldn't all have belonged to his ex-wife."

"Anything specific that you can recall? Maybe some pieces of jewelry?"

"Nothing in particular."

"How about a heart? A silver heart? A pendant on a silver chain?"

"I don't know. It was a while ago and I was scared. I closed the drawer and got out of there."

"What was he like, this Micah Moore?"

"Good looking. Nice. Quiet and intelligent. I was surprised at first he didn't have a wife or a girlfriend."

"Because he wouldn't have trouble finding one?"

"That's what I thought. But then I found out he was divorced and had two grown kids who lived with their mother. And when I saw that stuff in his dresser I thought maybe it did belong to his ex-wife, you know. Then I realized, like I told you, the stuff came from a bunch of younger women. After that it felt creepy to be around him."

"And you didn't work for him or see him after that?"

"He called me a few times. But I made excuses."

"Does Micah Moore's house have a security system—cameras, alarms, that kind of thing?"

"I don't think so. He does have his dog, of course."

"What kind of dog?"

"Doberman."

"*Ugh.*"

"She's really sweet. Roxy is her name."

"Roxy, huh?"

"Yeah, for such a strange guy he has a really cool dog."

"One last thing, Silvie. At the end of our call I'm going to text you a sketch of a man's face. Would you have a look and let me know if it resembles Micah Moore? This sketch is from twenty years ago. So please consider that Moore could have changed over time. Just try to pick out features like the eyes and nose and mouth that still would bear some resemblance to his younger self."

"Sure. No problem."

"Mahalo! You've been super!"

I hang up and find the sketch on my phone, attach it to a text, and send it off to Silvie. I work on my sandwich and wait.

Silvie texts back in less than a minute. "Moore is a little heavier than the man in the sketch and has a beard. But he looks similar. Especially the eyes. I'll never forget his eyes. They always looked sleepy."

Sleepy eyes? I didn't see that myself in the sketch. But if she does, fine.

I text back a thumbs up emoji that doesn't begin to express my gratitude to Silvie.

Then there's another text from Silvie: "What are you going to do to Micah Moore?"

"I can't say at the moment," I explain, "but can I let you know what finally shakes out?"

"Cool," Silvie replies.

Micah Moore is my best lead so far. He's worth a drive to Kehaka, at the other end of the island.

twenty-three

I navigate afternoon traffic around Līhu'e and head west for Kekaha. Passing Kaua'i Community College on the way reminds me of Strangler victim Tara Marie Havens. Am I finally getting closer to her killer?

It's a relatively long drive from Kilauea to Kekaha that can take a couple of hours. I say relatively because though this is a small island I'm driving nearly from one end to the other. The highway runs mostly inland until finally reaching Kekaha, where it hugs the shoreline and a lovely little beach with sweeping views across the channel to Ni'ihau.

A former mill town, Kekaha is the last settlement on the West Side, bordering the Pacific Missile Range and Barking Sands Beach.

It's approaching evening when I arrive and the pink grapefruit sun is setting over Kekaha Beach. My lodging is a Kekaha B & B, a pole house on the beach with two separate apartments—one in which the affable middle-aged couple who own the place lives, the other where I'm staying tonight. I use their wi-fi to do a background check with my favorite search platform. In my business it's an essential tool, providing an overview of an individual, full name and variations and aliases, next of kin and associates, current and past addresses, education and professional training, business and financial history, defaults and bankruptcies, trial and arrest records, court orders, and more. Within a few minutes I can learn more about a person than some people who have known that individual all his or her life. Some things we just don't tell even our closest family and friends.

I key in the name Micah Moore.

After refining the search to this particular Micah Moore who lives in Kekaha on the Garden Isle, instantly I get Moore's current street address on Hale Koa in Kekaha. He's lived here quite a long time, back even before the Barking Sands murders. An online map shows his house on the bend in the road, just like Silvie described. He holds a high school diploma and has a few semesters at Kaua'i Community College. No criminal record. No arrests. No court orders. No defaults or bankruptcies. He likes guns. He posts on gun forums. That could be a potential problem in arresting him. But that's KPD's *kuleana,* not mine.

Moore is divorced, also as Silvie told me. His wife and two sons live in Līhu'e. He's worked in Garden Isle government for much of his adult life. At the time of the murders Moore's sister, Kay, was co-chair of the Kaua'i County Police Commission. Moore married and had two sons, which could explain why he, if he is the Strangler, went dormant for so many years. And his divorce could explain why he became active again. Maybe his being alone—no wife and no children—triggered him? If Moore is the Strangler and goes unchecked he could kill again.

Moore could fit the pattern Professor Strohmeyer outlined of someone who can pass as a normal person, even a trusted and respected public figure, and yet lead a double life—an individual apparently above suspicion.

Why would such a person kill? My trusted online source doesn't tell me that. It doesn't bring up a woman who may have jilted him as a young man. Or a wife who lied to him, cheated on him, or disgraced him. Or a parent who hurt him emotionally or physically or made him feel worthless or ashamed.

Recent photos of Micah Moore from the internet show a pleasant-looking bearded man in his mid-forties. He gives the impression of being someone a woman could trust. A good find on a matchmaking site. A warm and cozy date. Moore has regular, comely features similar to Boz: dark brown hair, greying at the temples, but grey rather than blue eyes. And his eyes, now that I study them more carefully, do look a little sleepy—corroborating Silvie's observation. Even with the few extra pounds Moore has put on he fits closely enough the description of Jennifer's abductor. This could be the guy.

Moore is currently employed in the county prosecutor's office which is inside the KPD headquarters building. He couldn't get much closer to law enforcement if he were a police officer himself. But he isn't. He isn't an attorney either. Still, he must know something about the law and legal forms and documents in order to hold down a position in the prosecutor's office. He doesn't appear to be a supervisor but rather someone who actually processes legal documents. In any case, he could have learned enough about the law and law enforcement to help him remain off the radar for all these years.

I see connections. Moore works for Prosecutor Kalaheo whom Newfield challenged and beat in the election. But what motive would Moore have to assault and murder Newfield's daughter? Wouldn't it make more sense to expose her? Wouldn't that discredit Newfield rather than elicit sympathy for him if his daughter became a Strangler victim? After all, Newfield had promised, if elected, to solve several cold cases, most prominently that of the Barking Sands Strangler. Or maybe Moore merely noticed Alana, an attractive young woman, around her father's campaign? Serial killers usually don't know their victims. But Moore's working in the Prosecutor's Office suggests a connection, even if slight.

Finishing up my quick research, I ask my hosts about a dinner spot in Kekaha and they inform me there isn't much. They recommend the Shrimp Shack in Waimea. I know the place. The Shrimp Shack is where I met Ronnie, Jennifer Reece's surfing buddy, at the beginning of this investigation.

On my way to the roadside eatery I swing by Micah Moore's address on Hale Koa Street, a curving asphalt strip of humble plantation-style cottages. Moore's house, it turns out, lies hidden from the street on a flag lot. On either side of his driveway are two overgrown properties populated by rusting vehicles on flat tires. Nobody stirring. I glance up his curving driveway to a small white dwelling and carport. The carport is empty. I assume Moore—and his dog?—are not there. Or maybe the dog is inside?

I have a good look around without calling attention to myself and then head to the Shrimp Shack. It's a local-style outdoor eatery with order and pickup windows and picnic tables under a tin roof. The place is humming. Another customer is picking up an order of golden deep-fried coconut shrimp as I approach. Looks good. I point and say, "I'll have that."

"Fries with it?" the perky local girl behind the counter asks.

"Fo' sure."

While I'm waiting for my coconut shrimp I remember something Ronnie told me. In his hunky Kelly Slater guise, he mentioned a guy Jen had dated named Mitch. Ronnie said he'd never met Mitch and never saw him. He informed Kaua'i police but they apparently couldn't locate Mitch. Micah and Mitch. Similar sounds. Similar spellings. Did Jennifer date the man who murdered her? Not if Moore followed the usual pattern of serial killers.

When I return to Kekaha my hosts are sitting on their deck looking out on the darkened sea. I drop Micah Moore's name and ask if the couple know him.

"Not well," the husband says. "Moore keeps to himself, especially since his divorce."

"And before then?" I ask.

"Years ago, we bought an old orange Beetle from him for our son. He's since graduated from college and is on the mainland now and the Beetle is long gone. It had nearly rusted into the ground."

An orange Beetle. I remember that Dr. Gwen Kalama mentioned one following Tara Marie Havens. I ask if they have a photo of their son with his Beetle.

Shortly the wife digs one up.

The VW's orange paint, by the time of this photo, had

turned flat brown, typical of a vehicle parked outside in the island's salt air and blazing sun.

"What happened to this Beetle after your son went off to college?" I'm wondering if this could be the VW that transported the Strangler's victims to their Waimea Canyon graves.

"We sold it for scrap," the husband says. "By then the thing was undrivable."

"Thanks."

"Why do you want to know?" his wife asks.

"I have a thing for early Beetles." This is true. I do have a thing for early Beetles. But they don't need to know that the Beatles I'm talking about are different Beatles.

"Oh," she replies.

"Do you mind if I snap a pic of your son's Beetle?"

"Not at all. I'm sorry it's not here for you to see in person."

I snap the pic and fortunately they ask nothing further about Micah Moore—although I'd like to know more about his Doberman.

Early Tuesday morning, I park on Hale Koa Street a few doors down from Micah Moore's driveway, sit in my rental car, and watch. There's now a vehicle in the carport, an older gray Toyota pickup. It's a weekday and before long Moore pulls out in his truck heading for, I assume, his job at the Prosecutor's Office. The bearded West Side man resembles his photos on the internet, greying temples and all, except he's wearing Raybans. The Doberman named Roxy does not appear to be with Moore, which probably means she's in the house. Bad news.

I sit in my car for some time. Thinking. Breaking into a home is risky. Breaking into a home with a Doberman is just plain stupid. Whether or not the dog attacked me, she would make a lot of noise. Not to mention, if I'm caught I could face arrest and potentially lose my PI license.

I could inform Nakamura that there is probable cause to search Moore's house. But Moore is well connected to island government—Nakamura no doubt knows him—and I'm a private detective, not a police officer, and from off-island. A hard sell. And I have only the word of a dog-sitter I haven't even met that Moore possesses mementos possibly from victims of the Barking Sands Strangler.

My only real option: Break in. And don't get caught.

After sitting in my rental car on Hale Koa Street for several minutes, with occasional vehicles passing, I get a potential break. A young woman in shorts and T-shirt, barely more than a teenager—another dog-sitter?—walks up Moore's driveway to his front door. She reaches under a doormat, withdraws a key, and lets herself in. A minute later she emerges with a sleek black Doberman Pincher. Roxy's cropped tail stands almost straight up.

The girl and the Doberman amble down the driveway and turn into the street. She gives me a long look when she passes by. I smile. She pulls out her cell phone and keeps walking. Moore obviously has an arrangement with this dog-sitter to carry out this daily routine. And who knows what else?

I step from my car and walk up Moore's driveway, scanning the plantation-style cottage and the humble dwellings on both sides of the street. There's no person in sight. And no traffic on Hale Koa.

I reach under the doormat, find the key, and slip it into the front doorknob. Inside, the place is spare—bare windows and walls and a tile floor with minimal furnishing and a large-screen TV. Its remote sits on a faux-wood coffee table next to a stack of gun magazines. No area rugs or curtains soften the hard surfaces. Well, except for stuffed dog toys scattered on the tiles.

I make a beeline to what looks like the larger of two bedrooms and then to the bottom dresser drawer, as Silvie described it. On of the dresser is a photo of a younger Moore with two boys, who I assume are his sons. Inside the bottom drawer I find women's undergarments in various colors and styles and sizes. All youthful. And costume jewelry. A turquoise ring. A gold bracelet. A tie-died blouse that I can imagine free-spirit Tara Havens wearing. *Bingo.* But I don't find Jennifer Reece's silver heart.

I hear a car cruise by on Hale Koa street. Something tells me I better wrap this up.

I keep digging.

Finally, under a beach cover-up that may have belonged to Jennifer, I find it—the locket inscribed with a J. It's in amazingly good shape. Untarnished. Bright and gleaming. Probably it hasn't seen the light of day for twenty years. I recall the two photos where I first saw this charm. One, carried always by her mother, showing Jennifer in her graduation finery in a gauzy airbrushed portrait. The other showing Jennifer wearing a bikini and sunny smile, her eyes sparkling with apparent fascination for the photographer himself. Ronnie took this pic on Polihale Beach just a few days after he met her. He admitted to me that by then he was already head-over-heels for her.

Once the silver locket is in my hand I don't want to let it go. This is key to my case—solid evidence that Micah Moore abducted and killed Jennifer Reece. The inscribed pendant should be found by law enforcement on Moore's property, along with the other items, to link him to the crimes. But isn't there enough evidence without the locket to make that link? And once the silver heart goes into evidence it may be a long time coming out again. Longer than Mrs. Reece even lives? I place the locket on top of the dresser and think on it.

Before closing the drawer I snap pics of the various pieces of evidence. And to connect this evidence to Micah Moore, I snap the photo of Moore and his two boys next to Jennifer Reece's silver heart. Then I slip the heart into my pocket. Now I've added robbery to unauthorized entry.

On my way out I open the wrong door—to a closet containing an arsenal. Guns and ammo, including a Soviet-era AK-47 assault rifle. I know what an AK, or Avtomat Kalashnikov gas-operated weapon, can do. I'm not a gun guy, and I think the world would be a better place without them, but circumstances have forced me to become familiar with a wide variety.

After I surfed myself out of college in California and that Army recruiter dangled a cushy job in Waikīkī, I found myself at Fort Ord in Monterey training for the infantry. Handguns, automatic rifles, grenade launchers, machine guns, wire-guided missiles. You name it, I shot it. And since becoming a PI I've trained on Glocks, Sigs, and Berettas, and my own Smith & Wesson .357 Magnum. At Fort Ord drill sergeants kept AK-47s around to show us recruits what we might be up against in combat. The AK was less accurate than our lighter-weight M16 rifles, but the Soviet weapon had more kick, carried a larger round, and at short range could knock a man down. I never wanted to be on the wrong end of an AK-47.

In other words, Moore is nobody to mess with. I snap a photo of his arsenal. Nakamura will want to know what she's up against.

twenty-four

I walk but don't run down his driveway and hop into my rental car. I pull from the curb and almost instantly a police cruiser closes in behind me—blue lights flashing.

I stop. In my rearview mirror I watch the officer open his door and walk toward my car. He looks vaguely familiar. I put down my window. He stops behind me and looks inside the car. He's standing back until he determines if I have a weapon. If I do, he doesn't want to be in the line of fire.

Once he seems reassured that I'm safe he steps forward. "Good morning, sir. May I see your driver's license and registration, please?"

I reach for my wallet and hand him my license. "This is a rental car," I say. "I'm not sure about the registration."

"Try the glove box," he says. Yes, I've seen his face before but can't recall where or when.

I check the glovebox and he's right. The registration is there. I hand it to him.

He studies my license and the registration. "Kai Cooke?"
I nod.

He peers at me and says, "Don' I know you, brah?"

I take a good look at his name tag. M. ZHAO. The West Side patrol officer introduced to me by Detective Nakamura.

"Sergeant Zhao, howzit?" I say, relieved. Is this my lucky day? I shift into Pidgin. I may not look local, but I can talk local when the situation calls for it. I grew up here and was *hānaied* by Hawaiian relations. The lingo of the islands is second nature to me.

"Eh, Kai, wot you doin' ova hea in Kekaha?"

"Workin' da Barking Sands Strangler case. Dat's why I bin talk wit' da Detective in Līhu'e."

"Barking Sands? In dis neighborhood?" He looks dubious.

"A lead. You know. Gotta follow 'em all."

Sergeant Zhao looks unconvinced. "Kai, brah, I gotta tell ya, somebody call in da license plate of dis car."

"Dis car?" I try to sound surprised.

"Dat's right, brah. One prowler in da area. One break-in artist, you know."

"Somebody t'ought it wuz me?" I raise my pitch, like I'm baffled.

"Guess so, brah."

"Nah! Mus' be mistake."

The sergeant glances up into the hazy blue sky. I think he's having an internal dialogue over what to do with me. The license plate number that's been called in is no doubt mine. And he may correctly suspect the prowler was me, working my case. But, counterbalancing this, he's got to wonder how well I'm connected to Detective Nakamura. And what the fallout might be if he took me in. Especially compared to the little harm done in letting me go?

The sergeant lowers his eyes back down to me. "Kai, brah,

you see anybody 'round hea lookin' suspicious kine?" He has to ask, but I doubt he expects much.

"Nah. But if I see 'em I gonna let you know."

"T'anks, eh?" Sergeant Zhao walks back to his police cruiser and turns off the flashing blue lights. He gets in, pulls around me, waves, and is gone before I start my car.

If any officer other than Sergeant Zhao had stopped me I might be riding to Līhuʻe right now, handcuffed, in a police cruiser. And then I'd be talking to a judge rather than to Detective Nakamura. I came within a whisker.

I call the detective's cell phone and leave a message.

"Aloha Detective Nakamura. Kai Cooke here. I've got evidence to share with you on the Barking Sands case. I'm going to email you some photos from a confidential source. I'll be at police headquarters in less than an hour to explain."

I want Nakamura to see the photos from Micah Moore's home, but I don't want her to know I took them. That would lead to awkward questions.

I send the photos to the email address on Nakamura's card. I don't explain the photos, especially Jennifer's necklace and the image of Moore and his sons. Or Moore's arsenal. When I see the detective in person I will connect the dots.

I pull away from Hale Koa Street in Kekaha, and head again to Kauaʻi's metropolis. Before long I'm at police headquarters and I climb the stairs to the second-floor. I'm glad to be climbing those stairs of my own free will—not in cuffs.

Stepping up to the intercom at Investigative Services, I identify myself and ask to see the detective. The receptionist remembers me.

"Is she expecting you?" she asks.

"She should be," I explain. "I called and emailed her about an hour ago."

"She's very busy, Mr. Cooke," the receptionist says.

"I need only five minutes," I say. "Please let her know I'm here."

I wait while the receptionist steps away.

"Five minutes, Mr. Cooke," she says when she returns. "That's what the detective can spare."

I get buzzed through. Nakamura's open sunny smile is hiding today behind a cloud.

"What's wrong?"

"Just another day in Investigative Services," she says. "Whatcha got?"

"Did you receive my email? And my voicemail?"

"I haven't checked either since early this morning."

"How about you check now?"

She walks to her desktop computer and opens her email program. My email, although it came an hour ago, is not on top. A dozen other emails have come in since. I can see why she feels swamped.

She clicks on mine and asks, "What am I looking at?"

"Evidence from the Barking Sands murders."

She scrolls through the photos. The articles of clothing. The costume jewelry. The faux-gold bracelet. The tie-died blouse. "What are these things?"

"Effects of the victims."

"Any items you can connect to Alana Newfield?"

"I don't know. I haven't been in the loop on that investigation."

"Can you make positive ID of any victims from any of this stuff?"

"Keep scrolling," I say.

She sees the most recognizable piece of evidence, the silver locket engraved with a J.

"Recognize it?" I ask, not mentioning that the locket itself is in my pocket.

She slowly nods. "Jennifer Reece. Where did you get this photo?"

"Confidential source," I explain. "But I can tell you that all this evidence comes from the Kekaha home of Micah Moore."

"Micah Moore?" she says. "He's worked in the prosecutor's office for years. What do you have that ties him to this evidence?"

"You mean other than the fact that it was found in his home?"

"The photos show evidence, but they don't, on the surface anyway, point to Moore."

"Keep scrolling."

She scrolls to the framed photo of the younger Moore next to Jennifer's necklace. Nakamura takes a long look. "Okay, I recognize both the silver heart and the man."

"Convinced?" I ask.

"How did you get these?"

"Confidential source, like I said. And let me give you a tip from my source. If you're going to search Moore's home you should scroll to the last photo."

She does and sees the guns and ammo. "All these in Moore's home?"

I nod.

"This is confidential, Kai. Micah Moore was once on our list, low on our list, since he bore a faint resemblance to the police sketch of the Strangler."

"Moore may be the West Side resident Ernie Hong was trying to remember," I say, "but he couldn't come up with his name."

"Staff in Prosecutors office back in Ernie's time apparently joked about Moore's likeness to the sketch. He laughed right along with them."

"And didn't Moore's sister serve on the police commission?"

"True. Moore got a pass. And interest in him evaporated over the years. I might have done things differently, but I wasn't here. By the time I arrived there wasn't much interest in the old list. New leads were wanted. And that's where the resources went."

"Understood. And if you need more evidence here's a photo of the vehicle Moore probably used to transport his victims." I show her the orange Beetle. "Dr. Gwen Kalama, Vice Chancellor at Kaua'i Community College, remembered Tara Marie Havens saying she was followed by a Beetle that looked like this one."

"Where did you get the photo?"

"From a couple in Kekaha who bought the Beetle for their son from Moore. The car is long gone. Only this photo remains as evidence."

Nakamura studies the orange Beetle.

"Moore would have been in his twenties when he owned this Beetle. If you look into Moore's earlier life you may find a girlfriend or even his own mother he's trying to avenge. The victims represented or stood in for this woman. You may also find that he was abused as a child. And lived in an atmosphere of abuse—his parents always after each other, and so on."

"I remember hearing about his parents," Nakamura replies. "His mother was a beauty. But an alcoholic. Her husband was abusive. They fought. He was arrested and she got a restraining order. But he kept coming back. Both children were put in foster homes for a time. And then returned to their mother who, by that time was in a very bad way. Eventually she went into rehab. I heard that people marveled at how well Micah and his older sister Kay came out, despite their abusive parents and chaotic upbringing."

"Maybe Micah blamed his mother?"

"Why not blame his father?" Nakamura replies.

"Makes as much sense to me, but Moore didn't target men; he targeted women."

"Another question: Why wait twenty years after his first three victims to kill another?"

"Did he wait? Or did he also kill Amity Johnson?"

"Even ten years is a long time between crimes," the detective says.

"Moore took time off to marry and raise a family," I say. "Now he's divorced."

Nakamura shakes her head. "And back at it again?"

twenty-five

The wheels of justice can on rare occasions turn quickly. The next day Detective Nakamura has a warrant to search the Kekaha home of Micah Moore. She informs me that the warrant will be served around 5:00 pm, when they believe he will be at his residence. She says in light of Moore's private arsenal the serving officers will be accompanied by a SWAT team.

Since I've spent another night at the Kekaha B&B less than a mile from Moore's home, I stick around. Nakamura can't invite me along. But I'm sure she won't be surprised if I show up and keep a safe and respectful distance.

Since Moore works in the County Prosecutor's office, he may already know about the warrant. I hope serving the thing doesn't escalate into a confrontation. The Strangler needs to be taken alive—to stand trial and answer for his crimes. Moore himself is the only one who can illuminate what happened. The families of the victims deserve at least that much.

That afternoon I turn into Hale Koa Street before the SWAT team arrives. I park a few doors down from Moore's home and walk toward his address. Peeking down his long driveway this is what I see: Moore in his carport with his Doberman loading a dresser drawer and gasoline can into the bed of his truck. There's little doubt what he's up to.

He opens the passenger door and Roxy climbs in. He walks—not limps—around to the driver's side and lets himself in. I remember ironman surfer Ronnie telling me that the man who abducted Jennifer limped. If Micah Moore is the guy, his limp was simply a ruse—a tactic to elicit Jennifer's empathy, of which she apparently had plenty.

I'm not going to try to stop Moore. The case belongs to Kaua'i Police now. Not to mention that I'm unarmed. If Nakamura and her officers don't arrive soon they may have a car chase on their hands.

Just then a blue-and-white van and three police cruisers pull up in front of Moore's address. The van disgorges a half-dozen SWAT team members in combat gear—helmets, face shields, vests, and assault rifles with banana magazines. They assemble at the end of Moore's driveway. Detective Nakamura climbs from one of the cruisers, along with other officers in blue. When Moore sees the police vehicles and personnel he grabs the drawer and gas can from his truck and darts into his house. Roxy is left behind in the cab.

I'm not supposed to be here, but I can't stand by and watch an innocent animal hurt in a potential conflagration.

I step down the driveway and call, "Roxy, come!"

I don't know if she will. But luckily Roxy jumps from the truck through the open driver's door, looks around, sees me and slowly steps toward my voice.

"Roxy, come!" I call her again.

When she's close enough I step up and grab her collar and walk her out to Hale Koa Street out of harm's way.

Meanwhile the SWAT team slowly moves in. An officer goes to the front door, knocks, announces the search warrant, and requests that Micah Moore open the door. The officer uses Moore's full name, but I wouldn't be surprised if he knows him personally. Or is at least acquainted with him. I recall Nakamura telling me that everyone at police headquarters knows Moore.

Will he answer the knock? Or will he resist? He must know that if his property is searched and the damning evidence discovered, he could spend the rest of his living days in prison. This could turn into an awkward scene. Or worse.

The warrant request is met by silence. Just then a thin plume of smoke rises from a side window. Gasoline. Matches. Is Moore burning the evidence?

A minute later the officer informs Moore again, this time with a bullhorn, of the warrant. The officer adds that if Moore doesn't comply they will come in by force.

Silence.

Smoke billows now from that side window. The burning evidence, if that's what it is, appears to have gotten out of control. The SWAT team backs away as the smoke darkens and flames appear.

Moore suddenly shows himself in a front window with his assault rifle. He sprays several rounds in the direction of the team. They scramble for cover and then return fire. Moore's house gets riddled. He drops out of sight.

Flames lick up the sideboards of the cottage, jump onto the wood shakes, and spread quickly over the roof. A team member radios the fire department.

The officers back further away from the crackle and heat of the fire. If Moore's cache of ammo gets torched it could blow the house into splinters. He's put himself in a fix. He can't survive long in this inferno. He'll either have to quit the house or go up with it.

I hold Roxy out in the street, away from the fire. She nervously eyes her blazing home.

Distant sirens sound—the fire department racing from its Waimea station.

The SWAT team retreats further, stopping just in front of Roxy and me. Moore appears for a second time in a smoke-filled window and squeezes off a few more rounds. The team returns a thunderous volley that rips out the window frame and tears through burning wall boards. Moore again drops out of sight. I've got to think he's done.

When the fire company arrives they group behind the SWAT team, well away from the house.

Flames dart into the sky. The roof collapses. Sparks fly. Waves of heat roll out into the street. Firefighters stand by. Moore's house is simply left to burn. I wonder about the ammo inside.

If the SWAT didn't take him out already, Moore can't survive the fire. Nor can the evidence from the Barking Sands murders. There will be little left of either but ashes.

And then it happens. Moore's ammo. First it sounds like popcorn. Pop!—Pop!—Pop! Then louder like fireworks—skyrockets exploding in flight. Police and firefighters take cover in their vehicles.

There's a long wait for the popping to subside. Even then,

nobody goes near the house. After the flames die down, only a few bare bones of the frame remain. It's too dangerous for firefighters and police to recover Moore's body and search for evidence. That will have to wait.

I lead Roxy to Nakamura and state the obvious—the Doberman has lost her master and her home. The detective takes Roxy and promises to care for her until it can be determined if family members or anyone else have a legal claim to her.

"I'll be going," I say. "You've got your Strangler."

Nakamura nods. "But not the way I wanted him."

"Not the way my client wanted him either."

twenty-six

The next morning back in my Honolulu office I deposit Jennifer Reece's silver heart in my top desk drawer and call Mrs. Reece. "I have startling news. If you're not sitting down, you may want to."

"I'm seated," she replies.

"The Barking Sands Strangler is dead."

"Dead . . . ?" She sounds confused. "What do you mean—*dead?*"

"I found him alive in Kekaha on the Garden Isle, but he was killed in a confrontation with Kaua'i Police and a house fire."

"Now he won't stand trial? And answer for his crimes?"

"Afraid not. I wanted him taken alive too. But I had no say."

"I didn't think it would end like this."

"The good news is the Strangler can never hurt another young Jennifer. His reign of terror is over."

"Another death," she sounds despondent. *"Death upon death."*

"I'm sorry,"

"Did they find Jennifer's locket? "Her silver heart?"

"Yes. Her locket will be coming back to you."

Long silence. She starts to sob.

When Mrs. Reece hangs up I'm feeling down too—probably nowhere nearly as down as she feels. She was looking forward to her day in court—her chance to face the man who killed her daughter, prompted her husband's heart attack, denied her grandchildren, and essentially ruined her life.

Her day in court will never come. I'm sorry for her. Despite that I try to reassure myself with what I was able to accomplish—what law enforcement could not in twenty years. I solved the case with basic PI work. I had help, for which I'm grateful. I'm not expecting gratitude, but I know what I've done. Even if no one else does. I'm just sorry it's not, ultimately, what my client wanted.

Speaking of gratitude, I text Silvie with a brief explanation of what happened to Micah Moore and thank her for her help. Then I call Tommy Woo. He's been released from Straub Hospital. When I ask him about his condition and follow-up treatment, Tommy is vague.

"I'll be alright," he assures me. "The docs just wanted to poke and prod me. Didn't much increase my love for the medical profession."

"Oh?" I know Tommy isn't telling me all.

"It looks like Newfield got his man," Tommy says.

"So it appears," I reply. I'll tell him the real story when he's feeling better.

"Got his man," Tommy says, "but he may not get the Kaua'i County Prosecutor's office, if the recount doesn't go his way."

"That would be a double blow—losing both his daughter and the election."

"Newfield strikes me as the type who wouldn't let that happen. I told you about my dealings with him."

"You did," I say. "You're not just down on him because he didn't like your jokes?"

"Nah, I get that all the time," my attorney friend admits. "Remember I told you Newfield wanted me to find him a Honolulu agent who would track a defendant's car?"

"Yeah. No big deal."

"Well," Tommy explains, "the big deal was that Newfield wanted to attach a tracking device."

"Oh, now I see why you didn't call me."

"It's illegal, you know, without the car owner's consent."

"And why would anyone in their right mind give consent?"

"Exactly."

"Thanks for passing me by on that one, Tommy."

Wednesday morning, the Honolulu paper carries this headline:

KAUA'I MAN PRESUMED TO BE STRANGLER DEAD

Kaua'i Police believe they have captured and killed the notorious Barking Sands Strangler. Micah Moore, who burned to death yesterday in his Kekaha home, appears to be the long-sought serial killer. The Strangler went on a murderous spree twenty years ago that left three young women dead. On a tip Garden Isle police obtained a warrant to search Moore's property yesterday. Moore barricaded himself and torched his home and potential evidence from the murders.

With the blaze spreading, Moore discharged his assault rifle at officers. They returned fire and Moore sustained multiple fatal injuries. Before officers could enter, however, the home was consumed by flames. Kaua'i Fire Department rushed to the scene but was prevented from subduing the blaze due to exploding ammunition on Moore's property.

The story goes on. But there's no mention of officers recovering any of the torched evidence from the two-decade-old murders. Or of the most recent murder of Alana Newfield. Nonetheless, the prosecutor-elect goes on record saying he got his man, even though Newfield wasn't personally involved in the arrest. His campaign promise has already been fulfilled, despite a continuing recount that could call his election into doubt.

"My daughter's killer is dead," Newfield is quoted. "I would have preferred he stand trial and face the families of the young women whose lives he had violently torn asunder, but at least the case is closed and the island of Kaua'i can rest assured that the Barking Sands Strangler roams no more."

I leave a phone message for Mrs. Reece at her Waikīkī hotel. I want to give her Jennifer's locket.

My cellphone rings. Not Mrs. Reece, but Newfield.

I let the call go to voicemail. I can't bring myself to talk to the man, much as I feel for his loss.

Later I play his message: "Aloha Kai. This is Kaua'i Prosecutor Janson Newfield. Thanks in part to your investigation the Barking Sands Strangler, the murderer of three innocent young women twenty years ago, another woman ten years later, and only in these past few weeks my own beloved daughter has finally answered for his crimes. Our family will never be the same without Alana—our nightmare will never be over—but the Island of Kaua'i can now breathe easier."

And Newfield can now take credit for erasing one of the most notorious cold cases from KPD's blotter. If his thin election victory holds.

By afternoon I haven't heard back from Mrs. Reece. I'm concerned and call again to no answer. So I stop by the Regency Waikīkī with Jennifer's silver heart in my pocket. An aloha-shirted desk clerk calls her room. Still no answer. I ask him to have someone check on her.

After some negotiation it happens. I wait in the lobby. Finally, the clerk tells me: "I've got some bad news. They found her unresponsive in bed with a bottle of sleeping pills. We've called EMS."

Later I watch the emergency crew wheel a stretcher from a hotel elevator and into their waiting ambulance. On the gurney Mrs. Reece is unmoving. Only her colorless face is visible.

"How's she doing?" I ask a crew member.

He shakes his head. "You can check later at Queens."

"Was there a note?" I ask.

"A note?" He looks confused.

"A suicide note."

"Uh . . . we didn't see one."

He closes the rear doors and the ambulance pulls away. Lights flashing. No siren.

By the time I get to my car the ambulance is long gone. I drive to Queen's Medical Center and head to the Emergency Department and Trauma Center. I don't get much information from the staff about Marian Reece. I'm asked if I'm a family member. I tell them who I am—the closest thing to family Mrs. Reece has in Hawai'i. Even if I was family I doubt there would be much information yet. The place is jumping. And the trauma docs must be working furiously at the moment trying to revive her.

I take a seat in the waiting room. In my pocket I feel Jennifer's locket and fear her mother may never see it again. I ask every fifteen or twenty minutes about the patient. Still no information.

Finally after an hour it's growing dark outside and a petite woman touches me on the shoulder. She's in scrubs and looks tired and weary. "Mr. Cooke, I'm Dr. Sato."

I rise. "What can you tell me about Mrs. Reece?"

"I'm sorry," the doctor replies. "She didn't make it."

I lower my head.

The doc goes on. "By the time she arrived I'm afraid it was too late. We did everything we could."

I slowly nod.

"I'm so sorry." Dr. Sato returns her hand to my shoulder.

I look up again.

"If there's anything we can do—"

"Thank you for telling me."

I manage to walk from Emergency and Trauma to my car. I slide into the driver's seat and wonder where I am and where I'm going.

Thursday morning on Maunakea Street I'm still feeling adrift about Marian Reece. But no longer surprised. I recall her telling me the day we met that once she found Jennifer's killer she could die in peace and spend eternity with her daughter. The Strangler standing trial would have given her reason to go on. With him gone, her mission had ended. And all that remained was release from her unrelenting pain.

I wish I could have given Mrs. Reece Jennifer's silver heart. Would it have made any difference? Would it have kept her alive?

Then I realize the additional sad fact that Mrs. Reece has died before paying me. I rock back in my chair and gaze out the window at the rustling coconut palms. *No good deed goes unpunished.* I'm doubly glad Matt Ossendorfer is waiting in the wings.

As I ponder my unpaid expenses in the Barking Sands case, a nagging question won't leave me: has my finding the Strangler also solved the murder of Alana Newfield?

The more I think about it, the more questions remain. In some ways Alana's death fits the pattern of the earlier ones—the Strangler signature, grave in Waimea Canyon, and presumption of sexual assault. Though not exactly. She had cigarette burns in the shape of a wave on her chest. But why was her body so poorly hidden in the canyon that it was found quickly? And why was the semen detected on her clothes from someone other than the Strangler? If not sexual assault, what was his motive?

I don't share Janson Newfield's confidence that his daughter's killer has been brought to justice. But if not Moore, who? Korgan Lew, the sex offender on parole? Kaua'i Police have no doubt grilled him already. Maybe another of Alana's customers? Not Boz. He's in the clear. But someone else on that fated Halloween night? And why would any of these leave the Strangler's signature?

I'm not in a position to investigate further, as much as I'd like to. Too many unpaid bills. And Ossendorfer's case, when it finally starts, will give me little time for anything else.

Friday morning Tommy Woo phones. He sounds somber. He doesn't even tell a joke.

"You okay, Tommy?" I ask. "Results from your lab tests come in yet?"

Tommy ignores my question. "Sorry to hear about Jennifer Reece's mother."

"You and me both. Had the Strangler survived she might still be alive too."

"Sad." Tommy still sounds glum.

"Sure you're okay?"

"Actually, Kai, I'm afraid I've got more bad news."

Uh-oh. Is Tommy's prognosis even worse than we thought?

"Matt Ossendorfer just called me. The Detroit case settled out of court. The plaintiff's attorney had second thoughts about going to trial. He got a boatload of money for his disabled client. And that's the end of it."

"No Ossendorfer case?"

"Sorry, my friend."

It feels like a gut-punch. I don't know what to say.

"Kai?" Tommy sounds concerned.

"Mrs. Reece died before paying me. She stiffed me— unintentionally, of course."

"You need a loan? I know you're good for it."

"Thanks, Tommy. I'll be okay."

After Tommy's call, rather than dwelling on the additional bad news, I phone an acquaintance who works for a company that provides autopsies for Queens Medical Center. I ask which mortuary received Marian Reece's body. That kind of information can be tricky to get unless you're a family member of the deceased or you have power of attorney. After some delay comes the answer: Aloha Funeral Home. I know the director. And the facility is on Vineyard Boulevard, only two blocks up Maunakea Street.

I open my desk drawer, remove Jennifer' silver heart, and walk it to the funeral home. On the way I remember that Jennifer's surfing buddy Ronnie told me he would cherish this keepsake, if it were ever found. Ronnie still misses his lost love. And he helped me in the investigation. Plus, he's alive and Mrs. Reece is dead. But something tells me this locket belongs to Jennifer's mother.

At the funeral home I tell the director about Marian Reece and her daughter. He doesn't need convincing. He promises that the deceased will wear Jennifer's silver heart when prepared for cremation.

Walking back to my office, it feels like a weight has been lifted from my shoulders. I'm not thinking at the moment about my unpaid expenses. Or about Ossendorfer. I feel I've done right by Mrs. Reece. But then a more melancholy mood comes. Visiting the funeral home for some reason brings back memories of my own parents' death. And of Pono's.

When my mom and dad suddenly disappeared from my life it was a comfort to have Pono, my sunny mixed-breed or *poi* dog who looked a little like Kula. Pono's ears half stood up like a shepherd's and half hung down like a retriever's—in a homely, adorable way. He and I were inseparable.

After my father's rented airplane crashed into cloud-shrouded Mauna Kea on the Big Island, the tallest mountain in the Pacific, my Auntie Mae told me I mustn't worry about him and my mother because they had gone to a wonderful place, more wonderful than I could ever imagine. She explained that I wouldn't see them again in this life, but if I were a good boy and lived a good life I would see them in the next. My father, mother, and I would all live happily ever after together for eternity. That sounded pretty good to my eight-year-old ears. But the eternal happiness didn't seem quite complete.

"What about Pono?" I asked about my one remaining link to my parents. "Will he live with us in that wonderful place, too?"

She hardly skipped a beat. "Is Pono a good dog?"

"The best," I proudly said.

My Auntie tried to smile through her tears. "Yes, Pono will be there with you."

I was relieved. But I didn't know at the time how soon Pono would be going.

When I left the Kealohas to join my Uncle Orson's family in California, Auntie promised to take care of Pono until I got settled and then ship him to me. After a few weeks, my uncle got a call from O'ahu. He sat me down at the kitchen table, a somber expression on his face. "I have some sad news for you, Kai. Your dog was run over by a car. He didn't survive."

Pono's death, coming on the heels of my parents'—and without my Auntie's renewed promises of heavenly bliss—was almost too much to bear. Later she sent me Pono's collar and dog license. I think I still have them somewhere among my things.

I guess I shouldn't be surprised that Mrs. Reece's abrupt and unexpected departure brings back memories of Pono and my parents. But unlike my mother and father, my late client apparently made no provision for me.

Back on Maunakea Street I sort the afternoon mail and find an envelope from the Regency Waikīkī. Mrs. Reece must have posted it shortly before she took her own life.

"I've gone to join Jennifer," her note says. "Don't be sad for me. My suffering is over. My eternal joy begins."

The envelope contains a check. Mrs. Reece has paid me.

She has *over*-paid me.

twenty-seven

Saturday morning over coffee Vivienne and I talk about my late client. Viv isn't showing yet. And she's feeling fine. Kula is curled up beside us.

There's still a sadness in the air about Marian Reece, even as I share with Vivienne my doubts that the Barking Sands Strangler was responsible for Alana Newfield's abduction and murder.

"Is a Strangler copycat roaming the Garden Isle? Even though everyone on Kaua'i including the Prosecutor-elect assumes Moore did it?"

"What do you think?" Vivienne replies.

"My gut tells me Moore didn't do it. And my conscience tells me Mrs. Reece would want me to return to Kaua'i and find out who did."

"Then book your flight," she says. "You've been overpaid by that poor woman, you've got no new cases going, and you're determined to set the record straight."

"*Hmmm.* You make it sound so clear."

Viv shakes her head and smiles. "I say back to you what you tell me . . . and you think it's brilliant."

Monday morning, I hop a plane back to Līhuʻe and ask Detective Nakamura if her lab techs have found evidence that Moore killed Alana Newfield.

"You saw his house on fire, Kai," she says. "What do you think?"

"Not much left?" I state the obvious.

"Other than the images you sent me from your phone, we've got next to nothing. I would have thought Jennifer Reece's silver locket in the photo her mother showed us would have survived the fire—that is, if Moore didn't scuttle it before we came for him."

I inwardly cringe. "The photos displayed mementos from his three victims twenty years ago. Nothing from the recent murder."

The detective nods.

"Then we can't rule out the possibility that someone else killed Alana, mimicking the signature of the Barking Sands Strangler?"

"More likely to explain the ten-year-old murder of Amity Johnson that way."

"Then why not Alana Newfield?"

"Alana bore the signature," Nakamura says. "Who would go to that trouble and have that knowledge?"

"Someone in the know."

"To copy the MO of the Strangler would require a high degree of sophistication. Not just to burn the crude wave itself, necessarily, but to get everything else right."

"A killer with a powerful reason to make the copycat crime look like the real thing?"

"Maybe in Moore's twisted mind an assault on Alana

meant an assault on Newfield himself, whom Moore was afraid would become prosecutor. He could have feared that Newfield's election meant new scrutiny of him as a Strangler suspect."

I shake my head. "Not the same motive as the earlier murders? It's doubtful he knew his victims." I wonder if Nakamura is skeptical too, just not saying so.

She presses on. "Moore may have known Alana by sight, given her father's high-profile campaign. He may have even met her. Newfield himself thinks so but can't remember exactly when. So she wouldn't have been alarmed by him, say, if he came up to her."

"Do you have surveillance shots of Moore that Halloween night in Princeville?"

"No. But we do have Alana walking toward the dim parking lot, alone. So let's say Moore meets Alana that night, avoiding security cameras, gets her in his pickup, quickly subdues her, and takes her to Waimea Canyon, as he did the other victims."

"Did you find evidence of Alana and her assault in his truck?"

"Our techs are working on it. Moore was smart. We haven't ruled out that he used another vehicle, not his own."

"What vehicle?"

"We don't know. He could have borrowed or stolen a vehicle. We've put out feelers, but no luck so far."

I raise my brows.

"We have no one else, Kai. No suspects. And no motive for the crime. That leaves Moore. And that's where the department is focusing at the moment. Do I have doubts? Sure. But where can I go with them?"

"What about others on your Strangler list—like Joel Merryweather and Stephen Kahale?"

"We checked on them. They're both still on the mainland. Neither has been in the islands for years."

I leave Nakamura's office wondering where to start. Korgan Lew, with his history of violent crime and sexual assault, has always held a top spot on KPD's list. And he's out on parole. Of course he's been interviewed before. But now that the capture and death of Micah Moore has seemed to solve the Barking Sands murders, Korgan Lew must be old news to law enforcement. Not to me.

I drive north on Kūhiō Highway from Līhuʻe about a dozen miles to Anahola, where oceanfront palaces hug a tree-lined bay and more humble dwellings occupy Hawaiian Homelands in the valley behind. Korgan Lew's inland cottage can certainly be called humble. With all manner of stuff piled on the *lānai* the place looks like a pawn shop. I navigate the debris and knock on the door.

No answer.

I call his name: "Korgan Lew?"

Nothing.

He's either gone or he doesn't want to talk to me. Then I hear something crash inside the cottage. Maybe I'm in luck? Somebody slowly opens and says, "Whatcha wan', brah?"

He looks to be in his forties, medium height, in shorts and a tank top. He's got meaty arms and a thick neck like a snapping turtle. Bloodshot eyes suggest he's been burning the candle, or something else, at both ends.

"Korgan?"

"Yeah." He frowns. "Why you wanna know?"

"Kai Cooke, private detective." I hand him my card.

He doesn't even look at the card. "I already talk wit' da police."

"I'm not da police," I say. "I jus' wanna know what happen to Alana Newfield. Maybe you like help me?"

He shakes his head. Then says grudgingly, "Awright, c'mon in."

Inside the cottage looks like a hoarder's paradise. Stuff is pilled everywhere. I sit on a wood crate full of yellowed plastic dishes that rests on the plank floor.

Korgan parks himself on a rickety stool missing a leg. He starts off defensive. "Tol' you, brah, I already talk wit' da cops. *Twice,* brah. Da day aftah she disappear. Den da day aftah they wen' fin' her dead."

"What you tell 'em?"

"Not'ing. Dey try to pin 'em on me, but no use."

"You t'ink Micah Moore did 'em."

"Dat's 'im, brah. He da guy. He do 'em all—twenty years ago and today."

"Wanna know what I t'ink?"

"Shoots." Korgan shrugs.

"I t'ink da Strangler *make* da t'ree wahine tweny years ago. But he no *make* Alana Newfield. Her killer still on da loose."

"Wasn't me, brah. Like I tol' da cops awready. Wuz hea on Halloween. Nevah lef'. An' no way I gonna burn one wave on one wahine, brah. Dat's nasty. Dat's pervert. Dat's not me."

Korgan Lew has his standards. Copying the signature of the Barking Sands Strangler is beneath him. He would do things his own way.

"Den who *make* her like da Strangler?"

"Doan know, brah," he says. "Maybe you ask da new Prosecutah, her faddah, yeah?"

"Janson Newfield?"

Korgan nods. "He talk like he know everyt'ing."

"Yeah, but Newfield t'ink da Strangler did 'em."

Dat's what he *say,* brah." Korgan rises from his stool.

Leaving his cottage I wonder why Korgan Lew mentioned Newfield. Could Lew know something I don't? Or was he just throwing words around—uttering the name of the man he may believe is responsible for his recent hassles with police?

Back in my rental car my phone dings. An email from Seattle PI Kitty Stockwell. As promised, Kitty has sent court and other documents concerning Alana Newfield's arrest and hearing. There's nothing surprising in the court docs, but what does turn my head is a PDF copy of an invoice showing Alana's attorney fees paid by her own father.

Newfield knew all along about his daughter's activities in Seattle. And, therefore, he also knew why she left Saint Ursula College—not because of a traumatic breakup with her boyfriend, as he told me, but because she was booted out after her arrest for prostitution. Her light sentence—probation— may have something to do with Newfield's influence and the premium he paid for her legal representation.

Why didn't Newfield tell Kaua'i Police? Or me?

twenty-eight

I call Newfield's home and get his wife, Margaret Anne. Her voice still sounds weak, barely audible. I express my condolences again and ask if I might speak with her one last time about Alana. Mrs. Newfield agrees. She doesn't ask why I'm still on the case. That saves me a contorted explanation.

I drive up Kūhiō Highway to the Newfields' secluded acres in Kilauea. Mrs. Newfield's face is fixed in an expression that has hardly changed since I saw her last. She still seems to be absorbing her daughter's death—progressing, if at all, from stunned to numb.

I start by asking about Halloween evening.

"When Alana didn't return that night," Mrs. Newfield explains, "my husband called a family friend whose daughter, Nani, was to attend the Halloween party with Alana. Nani said Alana didn't go to the party. She had called to cancel earlier in the day."

I know why she canceled. The same reason she was arrested in Seattle and bailed out by her father. If her grieving mother doesn't know these things, it's not up to me to tell her. Mrs. Newfield no doubt would want to remember Alana in a better light.

"Thanks," I say. "What happened next?"

"My husband went looking for her in his Mercedes. Alana had been driving my Honda. And he hoped to spot the car. But he gave up after an hour or so, once he ran out of places to look."

"When he returned home without her, what time was it?"

"I don't remember."

"How do you know he was gone an hour if you don't remember what time it was?"

"Well, it seemed like an hour."

"Did you talk with him when he returned?"

"Truth is," she admits, "I was asleep. I'm surprised I could sleep on that horrible night, but Alana was only late at that point, not missing. And I had taken sleeping medication earlier."

"So you weren't awake when he came home?"

She nods. "Janson told me the next morning he had been out about an hour. He looked for her, he couldn't find her, and he came home."

"Is there ever anyone else—besides you and your husband and your daughters—in the household? A housekeeper, pet-sitter, personal assistant, or trainer? Someone like that?"

Mrs. Newfield hesitates. "Oh, there's Mavis."

"Who is Mavis?"

"Our housecleaner. She comes twice a week on Tuesday and Friday."

"Did she come on Halloween?"

"Let's see. Halloween was on a Thursday. Mavis came the next day. Friday."

"What does Mavis usually do on Fridays?"

"She cleans, of course. And she does laundry."

"She did those things on the day *after* Halloween?"

"I was so occupied by Alana's absence that I didn't pay much attention."

"Would you be willing to put me in touch with Mavis?"

"Sure. I've got her number in my phone."

"Thanks. And how about Alana's high-school friend, Nani?"

"I have her number too. Just a minute."

Mrs. Newfield goes into her phone's contacts and comes up with both numbers.

After the interview I call Newfield's housekeeper, Mavis. She's home, willing to see me, and gives me directions to her Kapaʻa home. I hop back onto Kūhiō Highway and head south. Traffic is light but starts to bunch up around the tourist mecca on the Coconut Coast. Colorful Kapaʻa is known for its Kauaʻi-made ukuleles, hand-crafted souvenirs, numerous *heiau,* and Nounou, or Sleeping Giant Mountain. Me, I'm bound for a home off the tourist track.

I cross the Kapaʻa Stream bridge and drive *mauka* or inland through lush green country for better than a mile. Mavis's place is a faded yellow ranch with one royal palm in front and two pickup trucks parked on the gravel driveway. A rusty chain-link fence surrounds the property. She's stands behind a screen door as I pull up and invites me into the modest and orderly island home. Ceramic tiles on the floor. Crucifix on one wall.

We sit on rattan furniture in her living room. I give her my card and ask about the Friday after Halloween at the

Newfields.

The spry grandmother—photos of her children and grandchildren surround the crucifix—scans my card and hesitates.

"This is off the record." I try to reassure her. "Anything you say will be held in strictest confidence. I'm doing this for Alana."

"Well, sir, on Friday morning I did notice something unusual in the laundry basket."

"What was unusual in the laundry basket?"

"The smell of cigarette smoke. I thought maybe one of the yard men had left his smoky t-shirt and Mrs. Newfield had put it in the laundry. He's always got a cigarette going."

"And was it the yard man's t-shirt?"

"That's what was odd. The smoky smell was coming from a shirt that looked like one of Mr. Newfield's."

"And you didn't expect that?"

"No, sir. Because Mr. Newfield doesn't smoke. At least I don't think he does."

"Did you ask Mrs. Newfield about it?"

"I didn't because Alana hadn't come home the night before and Mrs. Newfield was beside herself."

I ask more questions and Mavis does her best to answer, but after the interview ends the smoky shirt in the laundry basket stands out. The shirt may or may not have belonged to Newfield. If it did, the potential connection to the cigarette-burned wave signature of the Strangler is too suggestive to miss.

From Mavis's driveway I phone Nani, Alana's high school

friend. She wasn't with the Newfield's late daughter on Halloween night, but Nani mentions another friend of Alana who might have been.

"I've met Celeste only once," Nani says. "And Alana made sure her parents never met Celeste. When Alana returned from Seattle she hung out with Celeste more than with me or our other high-school friends."

"Why didn't Alana want her parents to meet Celeste?"

"Celeste does internet hookups. I think that's how she makes her living."

"You mean she's a call girl? A prostitute?"

"Celeste probably wouldn't use those words. But that's what she does."

"Do you think she brought Alana into the local trade?"

"Maybe."

"How can I get in touch with Celeste?"

"I don't know her number. I don't know where she lives. But you might find her on the internet at one of those hookup sites."

"What does she look like? Hair color? Eyes?"

"She looks kind of wild—bleached blonde hair with magenta stripes. Dark eyes. Thin and sexy. I can see why guys would go for her."

"Anything else distinctive about her?"

"Tattoos on her fingers that spell L-U-C-K-Y."

"Lucky?"

"Yeah. One small letter on each finger. Of both hands."

"She must think she's lucky?"

"Could be. She's very confident."

I thank Nani and drive back down Kūhiō Highway to Kapaʻa. For a hundred bucks I snag one night at Old Plantation Inn, a local-style condo-motel on the Coconut Coast.

I use a desktop computer and free wi-fi in the guest lounge to look for Celeste. With no phone number or address or last name, I follow Nani's suggestion to search hookup sites. I feel sheepish peering at the semi-nude, provocatively-posed women and men who pop up on the screen, especially as hotel guests pass by. I'm probably not the first guy or gal to use this computer like this. But I have a different reason. The steamy images roll by.

Twenty minutes come and go. Am I striking out? Finally, after several false hits, I find the woman who can only be Celeste—magenta stripes in her bleach-blonde hair and tattoos on her fingers spelling "L-U-C-K-Y."

I email her: "At Old Plantation Inn in Kapaʻa tonight. LMK what time and how much. Mahalo."

Short and simple.

twenty-nine

Within minutes she replies: "Tonight at 9:00. $200/half hour. $400/hour. I'm worth it."

I send her my room number. Then I get dinner, walk the beach, stop by an ATM machine, and call Viv and tell her about my evening plans.

"Tell Celeste hello from your pregnant girlfriend," Vivienne says.

We both laugh.

I go back to my room and wait. Nine comes and goes. No Celeste.

By 9:15 I'm thinking I've been stood up. Then there's a knock on my door. I open to the smiling blonde.

"Hi-ya," she says.

I'm about to make my awkward explanation.

She stops me. "You have the money?"

I pull ten twenties, fresh from the ATM, and hand them to her.

"Only two hundred?" She frowns.

"A half hour is all I can afford."

"Okay, honey." She swishes her hot pink bangs and climbs

onto the queen bed. "We'll have fun on your budget."

"Thanks, but—"

"No buts about it." Celeste reclines in an inviting pose. "I'm the best."

"And I'm a detective."

"A detective?" He dark eyes widen.

"Not a cop. A private," I explain. "I need to talk with you about a friend of yours."

"What friend of mine?" Celeste sits up.

"A late friend," I say, hoping she doesn't bolt with my cash.

"You mean Alana?"

"Just a little information."

"What do you want to know about her?"

"Halloween night. Anything you can remember."

"Okay. Alana and I both had customers on Halloween in Princeville."

"You *both* had customers?" Sounds like a break. "Tell me what happened."

Celeste gives me a censored version, I'm sure, about her gigs that night. And what she knows about Alana's.

"Did you see any of these men that evening?" I show Celeste photos and police sketch of the persons of interest in the Barking Sands Strangler case. I know already Boz was with Alana.

"I saw none of these men on Halloween night. But the guy in the sketch looks like one of my customers.

"One of *your* customers? What's his name?"

"Guys sometimes give me made-up names—or no names at all—so what they do with me can't get back to their wives and girlfriends. But this guy used his real name, I think."

"What was it?"

"Ian. He's a regular, when his wife's off-island. I think he lives in Princeville."

"Ian *Boz?*"

"Could be."

"You were with Ian Boz on Halloween night—the night Alana was abducted?"

"Yes."

"What would you say if I told you he was also with Alana?"

"I'm not surprised."

"Do guys do that often? Two women on the same night?"

"Not many guys," Celeste says. "But this guy thinks he's a stud."

"Really?"

She shakes her head. "I play along. I get paid to massage male egos."

"Hmmm."

"After Alana finished with her customer—Ian, from what you say—and was leaving the hotel she texted me." Celeste pulls out her phone and reads: 'Shit, my father's in the parking lot. He's getting out of his car and coming for me.'"

"What was he doing there?" I ask.

"I don't know. It wasn't really late. Not even eleven. It's a public access lot, outside the resort. No attendants. No security cameras. And Alana had a car, her mother's Honda. I replied to her: 'Why is he following you?' She texted back: 'You know why.'"

"What did she mean by that?"

"He was always trying to control her. She hated him. She didn't even think he was her father."

"Newfield was not Alana's father?"

"That's what she said."

"Did she explain?"

"She said she didn't look like him."

"That doesn't mean he's not her father."

"Not necessarily. But later she told me she had proof."

"Proof? What kind?"

"I don't know. She was running off to a hookup and never brought it up again. Anyway, I never heard from her after her text on Halloween. When I finished with my last customer and went to my car, her Honda was still in lot."

"May I see those texts?"

Celeste shows me her phone.

Sure enough, just as she said. "Could you forward the texts to me?"

"I could but I don't want my name or phone number on these texts."

"No worries. I'll forward them again to myself. Your number won't come up." I could ask her why she didn't go to the Kaua'i Police Department with this information. But the answer is obvious.

Then she says, "I want nothing to do with the police. If men want to pay me for sex, why should the cops care? Does the state want to tax me? Legalize my profession and I'll pay. But don't harass me and make my work more dangerous than it already is."

My half-hour with Celeste whizzes by and she flashes a sexy smile. "Next time let's play. I like you."

"T'anks, eh? You da bes'."

"I told you!"

She opens the door to a woman and a man waiting outside in aloha attire. They want to talk to us—to both of us. They are undercover cops.

I show my PI card and explain that I was interviewing Celeste for a case. It's the truth. But doesn't sound convincing. Even to me. The officers look dubious.

"Do you know Detective Nakamura in Investigative Services?" I ask.

The woman nods.

"I'm working with her on the Barking Sands Strangler case. This interview was about that case."

"The Strangler is dead," the male officer says.

"I know. I was in Kekaha when it happened."

"Then why are you still working the Strangler case?" he asks.

"I'm looking for a copycat killer."

The two officers glance at each other.

"Look, you've got no cause to hassle this woman or to hassle me," I say. "Nothing illegal happened in this room. And I'm sure Detective Nakamura will vouch for me."

They take a step back and exchange another glance. I imagine they're both wondering the same thing: *How well is this guy connected to Nakamura?*

After a moment's silence, the male officer says, "Have a good evening."

thirty

Lucky for me, Nakamura is a workaholic.

Saturday morning I talk my way into her office at Investigative Services. She's nursing a coffee and shuffling papers on her desk.

"I'm up to my elbows, Kai." She turns tired eyes to me. "Whadya got?"

"New information about Alana Newfield's murder."

"I'm listening." She continues to sip and shuffle.

"You might be surprised who it points to."

"I've got no time for suspense," she says.

"I think you should look at Janson Newfield."

"Newfield—our Prosecutor-elect?"

"If he survives the recount."

"Really, Kai?" She puts hands on hips. "You have Newfield killing his own daughter?"

"She may not be his daughter."

"How do you know?"

"A friend of hers told me."

"Would this be her friend you were with last night at the Old Plantation Inn?"

"You know about Celeste?"

"She's a hooker, Kai. You were intercepted last night by two of our vice officers. You dropped my name. They contacted me afterwards. Woke me up, by the way. Otherwise, you might be in a holding cell."

"T'anks, eh?"

"So, let me get this, Kai. A hooker claims our prosecutor's daughter is not his daughter, and you believe her?"

"Celeste said Alana had proof."

"What kind of proof?"

"I assume an ancestry DNA test."

"You assume? You don't know?"

"I'm sure we could find out."

"Even so, that's not much of a motive to kill someone."

"That wasn't Newfield's main motive. When Alana was arrested in Seattle for prostitution Newfield paid her legal fees. He knew what she'd been up to, despite not telling your investigators or me. When Alana began internet hookups on Kaua'i during his campaign, Newfield freaked. If she got caught his election prospects were doomed. Better Alana die at the hands of the Strangler, whom her father pledged to capture and prosecute."

"Kai, I don't like Newfield. Don't repeat that." Nakamura sips her coffee. "I wouldn't put it past him to do almost anything to get elected, but kill his own daughter?"

"She's not his daughter. Just look into it."

"Look into what?

"Besides Alana not being his daughter, Newfield's wife told officers her husband was gone only an hour the night Alana disappeared. But Mrs. Newfield doesn't know how long because she was asleep. He could have been out all night. He has no alibi."

"Or he could have come home in an hour just like he told his wife."

"There's more. Newfield's housekeeper, Mavis, on the morning after Halloween noticed that one of his shirts smelled of cigarette smoke. Newfield, though he apparently doesn't smoke, needed a lit cigarette to burn the Strangler's signature into Alana's chest."

"Or maybe he does smoke, but to protect his Mr. Clean image he doesn't want to be seen smoking. It's circumstantial, Kai. You've got nothing so far that links him to his daughter's abduction and murder."

"Try this," I say. "On Halloween night, minutes before she disappeared from the Princeville resort, Alana texted her friend Celeste that Newfield had come after her. He told your investigators he didn't find his daughter that night. Not according to Alana. He intercepted her at the resort, probably using a tracking device installed in the family's Honda."

"Do you have the text?" Nakamura asks.

"It's an exchange of texts between Alana and her friend. I'll forward them to you."

"How do you know Newfield installed a tracking device in the Honda?"

"It's in his bag of tricks. He asked my attorney friend in Honolulu to install one in a defendant's car."

"That's illegal." Nakamura sets down her coffee. "We can't even do it without a warrant."

"Newfield is the guy," I say. "We have three pieces of evidence that he abducted Alana: the blown alibi, the smoky clothes, and Alana's texts. Three reasons to look at him. The tracking device is icing on the cake.

Saturday afternoon I fly home to Oʻahu, satisfied I've given Nakamura what she needs to pursue Newfield. Now it's up to her.

On Sunday Vivienne and I go shopping for infant clothes— tiny t-shirts, shorts, onesies (whatever those are!) and other miniature apparel. Cute as the dickens. We don't know yet if the baby is a boy or a girl. So we don't shop specifically for pink or blue. Besides, Vivienne wouldn't hesitate to dress either a girl or boy in any color of the rainbow.

We get around again to discussing baby names.

"For a girl," I say, "how do you feel about Jennifer?"

"Like Mrs. Reece's daughter?"

"Yeah, to sort of honor her."

"Jennifer is the English version of the French *Guenièvre*." Viv pronounces it beautifully.

"*Guenièvre?* I like it."

"You do?"

"Uh-huh. Let's put it on the list."

Back on Maunakea Street on Monday I hear nothing from Nakamura. On Tuesday afternoon she finally calls.

"Kai, we served a search warrant on Newfield this morning for his home and office and vehicles," Nakamura says. "My investigators found a tracking device under the Honda and determined that Newfield traced the car to Princeville on Halloween night."

"How did Newfield explain?"

"He changed his story. He admitted he tracked Alana and intercepted her in Princeville, but claimed she got into his car voluntarily. He said she had been roughed up and bloodied by a violent client. He offered to drive her home, but Alana didn't want her mother to see her that way, explaining that she would drive herself home after she cleaned up. Newfield maintains that he never saw her again after that, until her remains were found near Koke'e."

"Did he give a reason for changing his story?"

"Yes. He said the first story was to protect the honor of his daughter and his wife and himself. And, of course, to keep the truth suppressed until after the election. On Halloween night he said he figured Alana would just clean up and come home. So he didn't even tell his wife he'd seen her."

"His second story sounds less likely than his first."

"Right. Nobody was buying it, not even his wife. She came unwound after her husband's backpedaling and changing explanations that made less and less sense."

"Do you have enough now to bring him in?"

"He's already in, Kai. We also found mud in his tire treads from Koke'e, which Newfield tried to explain. He claimed he motored up Waimea Canyon Drive only a few days ago, long after Alana's remains were found, to view the site again with his own eyes. He has nothing to corroborate that."

"Did he mention that Alana wasn't his offspring?"

"No. But his wife did."

"Really?"

"Here's the condensed version, Kai." The detective launches into narrative mode. "At the time of her wedding, Margaret Anne Bryan was already pregnant with her first daughter. Her future husband, Janson Newfield, was not the father. As Alana matured, she looked so little like Newfield and behaved so much like the footloose man Margaret Anne had dated before Newfield that she always wondered if he suspected. Fast forward twenty years. At St. Ursula College Alana took a DNA test for an ancestry research paper and discovered the truth. Alana then dove into Seattle's sex club scene, working under the pseudonym Sindee Sparks. Once she returned home to Kaua'i, after her arrest and getting booted from college, Alana confronted Newfield about her DNA matches. He wasn't as shocked as she expected. Alana also confided in her mother who, though she'd always known, was stricken by the news that her daughter had not only told Newfield but that he might have already known."

As I listen to Nakamura tell Alana's sad story, I begin to understand that her pain and suffering, leading to her reckless misbehavior, are connected to perhaps the even greater pain and suffering of her mother, who must feel some responsibility for her daughter's untimely and brutal end. All stemming from one bad decision in youth that Mrs. Newfield no doubt regretted for most of her daughter's tragically short life.

When the story wraps up Nakamura says, "Thanks, Kai. We couldn't have solved the Barking Sands case without you."

"Coming from you that's a colossal compliment."

"I mean it." She ends the call.

thirty-one

On the Wednesday before Thanksgiving, the Honolulu paper carries two stories that spell double trouble for Newfield. The first reports that in the election recount for County Prosecutor on Kaua'i incumbent Buddy Kalaheo has won. The second details Newfield's arrest for the murder of his own daughter. A sidebar says the decade-old murder of Amity Johnson is no longer being considered the work of the Barking Sands Strangler. Amity Johnson's death remains a cold case. Kaua'i Police will continue to search for her killer.

That afternoon I do something I've been putting off for weeks. I hop into my Impala with an empty suitcase and duffle bag and drive to my studio apartment at the Waikīkī Edgewater. With Vivienne and me living together and the baby on the way, it's time to turn in the key to my bachelor pad. Will I wish I could pop back when the sleepless nights of a newborn arrive? Maybe. But the Edgewater is ineluctably receding into my past. It will always hold my memories, but it can no longer hold me.

I drive to the soaring condo-hotel along the Ala Wai Canal in the backstreets of Waikīkī. Calling Waikīkī's tallest residential tower Edgewater is kind of a stretch. Unless you count the canal. The building sits nearly a half-mile from the beach. And I personally wouldn't put my little toe in the Ala Wai Canal. The warning signs are enough for me: KEEP OUT OF WATER. NO FISHING. NO SWIMMING. Better to amble across Waikīkī to its pristine rollers and famous white sands.

I park in the Edgewater's basement garage and take an elevator to the top—the penthouse level. After a long, slow slog with more passengers getting on and off than I can count, I exit with my suitcase and duffle and unlock my apartment door. My tiny studio looks like a closet compared to the sprawling penthouses that surround it with fabulous views of Diamond Head and the sparkling Pacific. Mine looks in the other direction at grey towers and, in the far distance, the Honolulu airport. While my neighbors gaze upon foaming surf and golden sunsets I watch jumbo jets lumbering down the Reef Runway.

My flat resembles a bargain hotel room with a kitchenette and teeny bathroom the size of a coffin at one end, and a small *lānai* with only a slice of glass between me and a thirty-five-story drop. Against one wall sits my double bed and nightstand. Against the other, a TV on the dresser, a photo of my late parents, and a surf poster. That's it. All that's missing to round out the tourist hotel effect are those tiny complimentary bottles of shampoo, aftershave, and mouthwash.

I haven't always lived in Waikīkī. I came here years ago from a cottage in Nuʻuanu Valley, off the Pali Highway. The landlord didn't renew my lease. Something about broken windows and bullet holes in the clapboards. The damage wasn't my fault, exactly. The shots fired from an automatic rifle missed me but riddled the cottage. After the landlord booted me I decided to seek the anonymity and round-the-clock security of a Waikīkī condo. Not to mention close proximity to Oʻahu's most consistent breaks and easy in-and-out for my flight attendant girlfriend at the time. Niki's airline provided free transportation between the airport and Waikīkī, stopping just a half-block from the Edgewater. Since her visits were typically short, the convenient location meant more time together. Or so I thought.

I open my suitcase and fill it with what's left of my clothes in the dresser and then gently slip my parents' photo between two soft cotton T-shirts. I roll up the surf poster and bind it with a rubber band. I fetch my few toiletries from the small bathroom. I unmake the bed and stuff the sheets and sole blanket into the duffle bag. As I pack up the last remnants of my things I consider what I'm leaving behind. An old photo of Niki in a bottom drawer brings back memories of her rare high-octane stopovers and the long, lonely nights in between. I'd wake in the wee hours to the pounding of garbage trucks plucking dumpsters in the dark alleys of Waikīkī. I also remember happier times of toting my longboard to the beach, surfing until sundown, and sauntering home in the afterglow, salt-glazed and stoked.

This was my single life at the Edgewater. My schedule was my own. When I wasn't working, I was surfing. And when I was working I was hopping from island to island on my investigations, as footloose as any wage earner could be. And so it goes.

I gather my suitcase and duffle and my surfing poster. I leave Niki's photo for the next tenant. Vivienne wouldn't appreciate it. I close and lock my studio for the last time. I pause at the door. I'm not sad about moving on. It's time. I ponder once more what will never be again. I had some good times here. And some bad times. More years will come and go. No doubt I'll look back on these footloose days fondly. Or maybe as just another phase in my life? Time will tell.

I lug my suitcase and duffle—stuffed with memories—to the elevator and catch a ride all the way down.

Late Wednesday afternoon, after stowing my things for now in my office, I drive to the Ala Moana Grand, a luxury resort on the edge of sprawling Ala Moana Shopping Center. Tommy Woo is subbing for another piano player on the early shift tonight.

The resort's main cocktail lounge is located just above street level overlooking a swimming pool whose deck chairs are still embracing sun-warmed bodies when I arrive at five. Inside the lobby a *koa* outrigger canoe on display gleams on the wine carpet. Beyond the canoe lies the sunken lounge with a bar and booths and grand piano.

As I step in Tommy is raising the fallboard over the keys. The lounge is all but empty, not surprising at this hour on Thanksgiving eve. I'm the only customer, aside from two well-dressed ladies in a booth rapt in conversation. I take a booth near the piano, give Tommy a wave, and order a beer.

Tommy is in a black blazer and black shirt, open at the collar. About as formal as he gets. He centers himself on the piano bench, pushes back that loch of silver hair that perpetually falls to tortoiseshell glasses, takes a breath, and launches into his first tune. I don't know all the jazz standards, but I've heard Tommy enough—both solo and with his trio—

to know his playlist. After the first few bars I recognize the sweet, melancholy, and seasonally-appropriate tune: "Autumn Leaves."

Tommy starts off slow and easy. He plays with a light touch, melodically and expressively, evoking the tune's nostalgic lyrics about lost love. Tommy is an artist. He once told me that a jazz pianist needs the reflexes of a surgeon and toughness and stamina of an athlete. And I would add to those the soft caress of a mother cradling her newborn child. To people who aren't musicians this may sound strange. It did to me, at first. But watching Tommy play over the years I've come to realize that it's entirely true. The piano under his sensitive touch—high notes twinkling and bass tones rich and vibrant—sounds almost ethereal.

I sip my beer as Tommy wraps up "Autumn Leaves." We make eye contact, I nod in approval, and after a brief pause he starts into another. I'm expecting this one: "The Shadow of Your Smile." Like I said, I know his playlist. And I know his musical idol, jazz pianist legend Bill Evans. After hearing my friend praise his hero to the sky, I once asked Tommy which Evans recording I should listen to first. Tommy didn't hesitate.

"Sunday at the Village Vanguard," he said, "a vintage 1961 live recording in New York City with Evans's first and finest trio. Paul Motian on drums. Scott LaFaro on bass. LaFaro died in a car crash eleven days after the recording. The three of them never played together again. This is the Bill Evans album you want to hear first."

Tommy finishes "The Shadow of Your Smile" and rolls through more standards. "Tenderly." "Body and Soul." Then he goes up tempo with "Take the 'A' Train." And slows it down again with "Misty." His improvisations sound fresh, even though he's played these songs hundreds of times before. That's joy of jazz, I guess, for those few musicians proficient enough to master it. And for those in the audience like me lucky enough to hear it.

Before long my beer is halfway down and Tommy announces he's taking a short break. He walks to the bar, grabs a cup of coffee, and joins me at my table. I notice up close that Tommy's full head of silver hair looks thinner than usual and his face appears slightly puffy, like an overripe apple. He's still projecting his avant-garde jazz vibe, but he doesn't look quite the same. I wonder if it's the effect of his illness, whatever it is, or the drugs he may be taking for it. Before I can ask how he's feeling, he starts the conversation off as he always does.

"Hey, Kai," Tommy puts on a wry smile, "what do you get when you cross an octopus with a turkey?"

I raise my arms in surrender. "I give up, Tommy." I brace myself for an off-color Thanksgiving joke.

"Finally," he delivers the punchline, "enough drumsticks for everybody."

"Tame," I say, "by your usual standards."

"I've got more." Tommy explains. "But Zanie says I should stop telling so many Thanksgiving jokes—"

"I see her point." I inadvertently interrupt.

"—but I told her I couldn't stop cold turkey." Tommy deadpans.

I shake my head. "Speaking of Zanie and Thanksgiving, can you two still make it to Viv's tomorrow?"

"Wouldn't miss it for the world," Tommy says.

"She'll be happy to hear that. By the way, I really enjoyed

your first set. You da bess, brah."

"Ah, shucks, Kai." He nearly blushes. "You shouldn't."

"I mean it, man. You've got a gift." I turn the conversation to what's been concerning me. "How are you feeling? Any results yet from the tests at Straub Hospital?"

"No worries, Kai. The docs pinched and probed me, but I escaped."

I peer into his averted eyes. He's not telling the whole story. I'm not offended. Tommy is Tommy. He's welcome to keep private whatever he wants. After all, I haven't told him yet that Vivienne is pregnant. I should just be glad he's not angry at my prying.

"Swell, Tommy." I respond. "If there's ever anything I can do, you'll let me know, right?"

"You already fed my cats when I was at Straub, Kai."

"And I'll do it again."

Tommy consults his watch. "Gotta get back to work. Anything I can play for you?"

I don't even have to think. "As Time Goes By." It's not a tune he plays often, but I know he'll play for me.

"You're an incurable romantic, my friend." Tommy replies. "You got it, as long as you don't tell me, 'Play it again, Sam.'" Tommy refers to pianist Dooley Wilson—a.k.a, Sam—in the movie *Casablanca* starring Humphrey Bogart and Ingrid Bergman, in which the song was featured.

"Promise."

Tommy rises, points at me, and puts on his best Bogart: "Here's looking at you, kid." My friend ambles to the black grand, leaving his coffee in the booth. He sits, gazes around the still nearly empty lounge, and begins to play "As Time

Goes By."

I don't know what chord changes he goes through. I don't have the words—the musical vocabulary. But I do know that the tune comes out subtle, provocative, mysterious, and beautiful. Tommy has a talent beyond my comprehension. He's a prize, that man. He's flawed like the rest of us—maybe even more than the rest of us—but he's a prize all the same. I sit in that booth and am transported by his playing.

After the last few measures of the song I rise and applaud. The two women in the booth look up startled—then they applaud too. Even the bartender puts his hands together.

I wave to Tommy and say, "Mahalo! I gotta go."

I head back to my car smiling but also worried. *I hope he's okay. I hope Tommy is okay.*

On Thursday, Thanksgiving Day, a few of Vivienne's colleagues join us for dinner. And, of course, Tommy and his girlfriend Zanie Moon. Before dinner I once more ask Tommy, still looking pale and puffy, about his health. He's evasive again. Then I pull Zanie aside.

She doesn't hesitate. "Tommy has lymphoma. It's a cancer that attacks the immune system."

I'm stunned. "Tommy didn't tell me."

"He didn't want to burden you, Kai," Zanie replies.

"Is he going to be okay?"

"Tommy's sure he'll be okay. He's getting chemotherapy. That's another reason he hasn't told anyone."

During dinner Vivienne announces she's having a baby. Tommy lifts his glass (of water not wine) and says, "To the new parents!" The other guests raise their glasses too.

"Well, it's out of the bag now," I say. And I glance at Viv. She's beaming. But of course not drinking either.

Later in the evening Tommy pulls me aside. I think he's finally going to tell me about his cancer.

"Hey Kai," Tommy breaks into a sly smile, "did you hear the one about the angry wife who kicked her husband out and said she hoped he'd die a slow, painful death?"

I have no idea where he's going. "Haven't heard that one, Tommy."

"The husband replied, 'So you want me to stay?'"

"Still cynical about marriage, Tommy?"

"Actually, I'm optimistic about yours."

"Mine?"

"You and Vivienne are having a baby, right?" He gives me a look.

"That doesn't mean we have to be husband and wife," I say, though I'd be ready enough to marry her whenever she's ready, despite our differences.

"C'mon, Kai. I'll marry you two."

"Marry us?" I chuckle inwardly that my twice-divorced friend should be such an advocate for marriage. Then I recall that Tommy performs weddings as a side gig. And I don't mean music—well, he does that too. What I mean is he sometimes plays the minister.

"Just go online to the Department of Health, fill out the forms, and pick me as your performer. You decide when and where you want the ceremony, and I'll be there."

"Shouldn't I ask Vivienne first?"

"You want her to show up, don't you?" Tommy winks.

thirty-two

Thanksgiving passes with the usual festivities and early the next morning, Black Friday, I arrive on Maunakea Street to a check from Acme Insurance. My photos and videos of the kite surfer have done the trick. Reginald Bowman has been outed for insurance fraud.

I've barely finished depositing Acme's check in my Surfing Detective account with my cellphone when my office phone rings. "Mr. Kai Cooke?"

"Speaking," I respond.

"This is Dave Sumner—Sumner, Bosco, and Peale Law in Colorado Springs. How are you today, sir?"

"Can't complain," I reply. "I'm avoiding shopping malls."

"Very wise. You know already, sir, that a devoted and long-suffering woman—Mrs. Marian Reece—passed away recently in Hawai'i."

"Mrs. Reece was my client."

"She had a difficult life." Sumner sighs.

"Yes, I know."

"I'm calling about her final wishes, Mr. Cooke. Mrs. Reece requested that her ashes be spread at Barking Sands Beach on the island of Kaua'i."

"I'm not surprised," I say. "She probably meant Polihale State Park—the last place her daughter was seen alive. It borders Barking Sands."

"We'll leave that up to you. The firm is prepared to pay your expenses from her estate. The rest goes to a foundation addressing violence against women and girls worldwide."

"Appropriate," I say.

"We thought so too," says Sumner. "Anyway, we've already contacted Aloha Funeral Home in Honolulu and authorized you to take possession of Mrs. Reece's ashes, whenever you're ready."

Sumner tells me where to send my expense report, he again expresses regret about Mrs. Reece passing, and is gone.

Once we're off the phone I call the funeral home to confirm that it's all arranged, as Sumner said. The director remembers my delivering Jennifer's silver heart for her mother. He reassures me that Mrs. Reece was wearing that necklace inscribed with J before she was ushered into the flames.

Since my calendar is clear on Black Friday, I book a late-morning flight to Līhu'e and a return that evening. I also reserve a Jeep. Then I swing by the mortuary and pick up a bronze urn and a certificate for airport security.

Before long I'm airborne again to the Garden Isle with Marian Reece's ashes in my lap. I pick up my Jeep and make that long, bumpy ride to Polihale.

I tote the urn across the wide beach to the spot where Jennifer Reece was last seen alive—before she was abducted by the man we now know was Micah Moore—the Barking

Sands Strangler. The surf today is roaring, like last time, and the dunes and the beach lie quiet under an overcast sky. Out in the depths, beyond the frothy shore break, the blue-black ocean reminds me of a darkness that can inhabit even a usually sunny spot like this.

I step up to where Jennifer was sitting on that fateful day. I open the bronze urn, scoop the ashes with my bare hand, and gently lift them into the offshore breeze. The ashes twirl in the air toward the water. As I release more into the breeze I recall when Mrs. Reece first told me about her mission. And how it soon became my mission.

When the last remnants of Mrs. Reece drift into the sea I take one last look at the beach, searching for Jennifer's imprint in the sand. I can almost see it.

I'm not a religious person. I'm not sure if anyone or anything waits for me on the other side. But if that's what Mrs. Reece believed, I hope she's there now—reunited with her daughter.

As I walk away I peer into the urn one last time and am surprised by what I see at the bottom. Jennifer's silver locket. It's untarnished. It's uncharred. I can only imagine that the funeral director couldn't bring himself to burn the lovely necklace. Or maybe funeral home practice is to remove jewelry before cremation? Whatever the reason, I pocket the heart and ask myself: *A memento for her lost love, Ronnie?* And then give it another think. *Or a keepsake for me?*

Of my first and definitely last serial killer case . . .

About The Author

Chip Hughes earned a Ph.D. in English from Indiana University and taught American literature, film, writing, and popular fiction for nearly three decades at the University of Hawai'i at Mānoa. His non-fiction publications include two books on John Steinbeck: BEYOND THE RED PONY (1987) and JOHN STEINBECK: A STUDY OF THE SHORT FICTION (1989). His published fiction includes six Surfing Detective mysteries: MURDER ON MOLOKA'I (2004), WIPEOUT! (2007), KULA (2011), MURDER AT VOLCANO HOUSE (2014), HANGING TEN IN PARIS TRILOGY (2017), and BARKING SANDS (2021). Chip and his wife split their time between homes in Hawai'i and upstate New York.